THE

Birthday Shoes

The Birthday Shoes

MARY WEEKS MILLARD

DERNIER PUBLISHING
Tonbridge

Book design and production for the publisher by
Bookprint Creative Services, <www.bookprint.co.uk>
Printed in Great Britain.

*I would like to dedicate this book
to the memory of my mother, Elizabeth Morris,
who enriched my life so much by both telling
and reading me so many stories
in my early childhood.*

Acknowledgements

My grateful thanks go to my patient husband, Malcolm, and to Janet Evans of Dernier Publishing, for all their support and encouragement. Without their help this book would never have come to birth!

ONE

The Birthday Girl

Emily Jane woke up early. She was so excited! This was her 11th birthday. She pulled back her bedroom curtains and looked out of the window. It was still dark. She wanted to put the light on and start to get washed and dressed, but she knew her mum and dad might be cross if she woke them up too early, so she went back to bed and hummed softly to herself: "Happy birthday to me, happy birthday to me, happy birthday dear Emily Jane, happy birthday to me!" Then she thought about the day ahead. She knew there would be presents and wondered what they might be! One thing she longed for was a pair of trendy high-heeled boots. Some of her friends had boots like that, and she did want some, too!

It was Friday, so Emily Jane would have to go to school as usual. She went to Windy Hill Primary School. It was about a 10-minute walk from her house, all up hill. She thought how great it would be to walk to school showing off her new high-heeled boots! She had invited her best friend Jenna to come to tea after school, and she was sure that Mum would make a special birthday cake;

hopefully chocolate, her favourite!

Emily Jane gave a sigh of happiness and began to hum to herself again. Surely her birthday must be the best day of the year!

As she was thinking all these nice thoughts, she heard noises in her parents' room, then her bedroom door opened and in came her mum, wearing a pink fluffy dressing gown, and gave her a big hug and a kiss. "Happy birthday, darling!" she said.

"Thank you, Mum," replied Emily Jane, almost jumping up and down in excitement. "Can I open my presents now?"

"Yes, of course," answered Mum.

Emily Jane needed no second invitation. She leapt out of bed and into the bathroom in seconds, and soon she was downstairs, ready to begin tearing paper!

Dad was sitting in his wheelchair, and there on the coffee table beside him were several parcels, presents and cards. Some of the presents were beautifully wrapped, some were in boxes with pretty paper and bows on the top.

The first present Emily Jane opened was from her grandparents and contained some lovely watercolour pencils and special drawing paper. "Mum and Dad, look at these!" she squealed. "I shall be able to do some fantastic pictures for you! They are much better than felt-tips. I can paint with them too!" Her parents agreed that it was a great present, and promised she could telephone her grandparents and say thank you later in the day.

Then Emily Jane opened a large box which rattled when she shook it! It contained a game from one of her uncles and aunts, about climbing mountains. It looked good fun and her dad promised to look at it and work out how it was played, so that she and Jenna could have a game after school.

The next parcel looked the size and shape of a shoe box, and Emily Jane's heart began to race – surely that must be the longed-for boots! She decided she would leave that one until last, and open another present that was near it. This one was from her parents; a DVD of *The Secret Garden*, which was one of her favourite stories. She was so pleased and ran to give her mum and dad a big hug each. "Thank you so much, I love it!" she cried. Then she began to rip the paper off the last parcel. It had been sent from Auntie Lucy who was working as a nurse in Africa. How did she know about boots? thought Emily Jane. Perhaps her mum had told her when they chatted on the phone!

Emily Jane threw the lid on the ground and pulled out the contents. To her horror, they were not boots at all, but brown shoes made out of a strange, shiny sort of leather, with a bar strap. Her face fell, and she felt tears coming into her eyes. They were horrid shoes! They weren't a bit cool or fashionable and she had wanted high-heeled boots so much!

Emily Jane's mum could see the disappointment in her daughter's face, but she asked to see the shoes. "Oh look, Emily Jane," she said encouragingly. "These are beautiful shoes, made to look like shiny crocodile skin. No one else in your class will have shoes like these. They are very special."

"I wouldn't be seen dead in those!" Emily Jane replied angrily. "I *hate* crocodiles and shoes that look like their skin! Why didn't Auntie Lucy buy me boots like everybody else in my class has? I am the only one who hasn't got trendy boots! Doesn't Auntie Lucy know anything about fashion? Girls my age wear boots, not shoes like these!"

She knew was being ungrateful, and also untruthful, because not everybody had trendy boots. It was just that she felt disappointed and cross because she had wanted boots so much. Emily Jane noticed her mum look at her dad, and they sighed. That made her feel bad. She realised that they probably couldn't afford them because since Dad's accident he had been unable to work, and Mum couldn't go out to work either: she had to stay at home to look after him.

"Never mind, dear, come and have your breakfast now, or you will be late for school," her mum said quietly, and Emily Jane tried to smile.

On Sundays they had a special treat for breakfast; a boiled egg. Mum had cooked one for Emily Jane this morning, even though it was Friday, and this cheered her up a little. Dad thanked God for providing food for them and also said a special prayer for his daughter on her birthday.

Emily Jane forgot about the shiny shoes until she was walking up the hill towards school, when it passed through her mind that she couldn't show off to everyone that she was cool, with high-heeled boots. An angry scowl passed over her face and she muttered to herself. "I *hate* shoes that look like crocodiles. I *hate* crocodiles!"

At school, during assembly, everybody sang Happy Birthday to her and also to another boy who was having his seventh birthday. That was very nice, and her teacher made her "queen of the class" for the day. It was fun to be made to feel special.

Mum had pushed Dad all the way up the hill to meet her and Jenna from school. She looked gratefully at her mum, who was a bit puffed with all the effort. It was so lovely to see Dad's smiling face waiting for her.

"How is my princess?" he asked, "Did you have a nice day?"

"I was queen of the class!" she replied, "But I am still your princess!"

Jenna and Emily Jane ran down the hill together, and again, Emily Jane felt angry thoughts pushing up inside her. She should have been running with new boots and have everyone looking at her, admiring them!

They were home very quickly, and the girls changed into their jeans and best tops.

"Are you going to try on your new shoes?" Mum asked Emily Jane.

"No, not today, they won't go with my jeans," she answered, thinking to herself, "I shall *never* wear them if I can help it!"

"What new shoes?" asked Jenna. "Let me see them."

"Oh, later," replied Emily Jane, not wanting her friend to laugh at the horrible shoes. Jenna rummaged in her school bag and brought out another present, wrapped in pink paper. Jenna had bought her pretty hair-bands and some make-up! Emily Jane was very pleased and the girls spent the time before tea doing each other's hair and make-up. Emily Jane's family had come originally from Jamaica, so her hair was very dark and curly. Jenna's was long, dark and straight. They had a lot of fun trying out different styles with the new hair-bands and experimenting with the new make-up.

After tea it was time for birthday cake, covered in gooey chocolate icing! As Emily Jane watched her mum light the candles on the cake, Emily Jane knew what she was going to wish for when she blew them out. Boots!

TWO

The First Adventure

The next day was Saturday so Emily Jane did not have to get up early for school. When she woke up it was getting light, but cold and frosty outside. Usually she loved Saturdays, but today she felt miserable. Her birthday was now over and deep down, although she knew she should be very grateful for her lovely presents and for having had such a lovely day, she still felt so disappointed about not having the boots she had wanted. She had thought about them for so long and wanted them for so long, it seemed almost impossible that she did not have them.

After breakfast she helped Mum push her dad to the shops to buy bread and milk, but all the time she was feeling grumpy. She looked longingly in the window of the shoe shop as they passed. There were no shiny, scaly shoes there! "I'm not surprised," she thought to herself. "They are so horrible, nobody would want to wear shoes like mine, not even grannies!" There were several pairs of boots in the window, though, and Emily Jane looked longingly at them. If only she had a pair like those she was sure she would be happy forever!

Once they were back home Emily Jane went moodily to her room. For a while she drew a flower garden with her new pencils, which cheered her up a bit. She was just about to get some water from the bathroom and use them as paints when she saw the box with the new shoes on the chair by her bed. She pulled a face and began to feel sulky and grumpy again. However, something seemed to make her curious, so she took the lid off the box and ran her hand over the top, feeling the scales. It made her think about crocodiles. Horrible creatures! Everything she had seen about them, in pictures and on the telly, had shown them as vicious creatures with big teeth, ready to crush and eat whatever came their way. Once, on a visit to a zoo, she had seen some real ones. She remembered thinking how ugly and menacing they looked. Emily Jane shivered and had goose pimples on her arms when she thought about them!

Then a thought occurred to her. "How does Auntie Lucy know what size my feet are? Maybe the shoes will be too small for me and Mum can give them to a charity shop, then someone else will have to wear them!"

That was such a good thought that Emily Jane decided to try on the shoes. Much to her dismay, the first one fitted perfectly! Then she tried the second, and once she had put it on, a strange thing happened! She found herself drifting away, not quite asleep and not quite awake. It was a funny, dreamy sort of feeling, and it felt good. It made her want to close her eyes, which she did, but as she opened them again she found herself standing by a huge lake, so big she could only just see the far side. The air felt warm, even steamy, and she was standing on a brown mud path!

"Where am I?" she asked herself in surprise, out loud. The trees around her seemed to whisper back, "Africa, Africa." Was she really in Africa? Emily Jane began to look at the trees around her. Some were covered with bright red flowers, others were spiky and spread out like a sort of umbrella. Then she saw some that had trailing things hanging down like long balloons. She was amazed and found herself whispering back, "Africa, Africa!" The sky was so blue, and everything around her so green and beautiful! There was also a sweet smell which she thought must be from the tree blossoms. Emily Jane listened and heard a sound she was not used to. It was the hum of insects. It was magic, like another world! It was so warm that Emily Jane slipped off her sweater and tied it around her waist. "I wish I was wearing shorts instead of my jeans!" she thought. "Wherever am I?" She looked down at her birthday shoes. "Maybe these shoes have taken me to my auntie in Africa!"

Emily Jane decided to explore along the path. There was no harm in that, she reasoned, and perhaps it led to Auntie Lucy's house. It was a bit difficult to walk along, because there was no tarmac, just red earth and stones, but Emily Jane managed to pick her way along without tripping. The path wound down towards the edge of the lake, where it widened out to reveal a few small, mud houses with tin roofs, right on the shore. The houses were more like huts really, with doors and roofs of corrugated iron and a small window on each side. Some windows were open; others were closed with wooden shutters, but none of them had glass in them. Outside the houses were small sheds. Emily Jane saw smoke rising from some of these and wondered if they might be kitchens! Near the houses were some canoes that had been dragged out of the water. The canoes were like hollowed-out tree trunks, each with a rough wooden paddle, not a bit like the yellow canoes she sometimes saw on the canal near her house at home. On a rack by the canoes fish were hanging up as if on a washing line. Emily Jane had never seen anything like that before, so she walked closer to get a better look. They really smelt bad and flies hovered around them!

A child came out of one of the huts and smiled shyly. Emily Jane smiled back. She was wishing she knew how to talk to the child, but was sure that he or she would speak another language. She wasn't sure if the child was a boy or a girl, and it looked about five or six years old. The child's head was shaved and it was wearing a long T-shirt that reached to the knees. Emily Jane was surprised to see that the child's skin was an even darker brown than hers. She was also very surprised when the child spoke to her in English.

"You like our fish?"

"I've never seen any like that before," replied Emily Jane. "Why are they hung up?"

"Now they stay and dry in the sun. They are good for a long time if they dry well."

"Oh, I have never eaten dried fish." Then she added, "What is your name? My name is Emily Jane."

The little child tried to repeat "Emily Jane", but found it hard, so just said, "Jane."

Then it said, "My name is Grace", so Emily Jane then realised she was talking to a girl.

"How are you?" she asked, very politely, for Emily Jane's mother had always insisted on good manners.

"I am fine," replied Grace. "I speak English well, yes?"

"Very well. Do you go to school?"

"I go to school and am in class primary two. We learn English in school. You go to school, too, Jane? I like very much your shoes!"

Emily Jane had forgotten all about her shoes and looked down at them. This girl thought they were nice. She was very surprised! Then she had a thought; maybe Grace could tell her where she was. She knew she had come to Africa, because the trees had whispered to her, but that was all.

"What is this place called?" asked Emily Jane.

"You don't know where you are!" Grace was most surprised. "We are near Jinja. It is a very important town. We have the Owen Falls Dam here. It gives electricity to all the big houses and factories in our country. This is

Lake Victoria and out of this lake flows the River Nile!" Grace pointed to the far end of the lake and Emily Jane could see what looked like a wall of concrete. She hadn't noticed it until Grace pointed it out, but she could see that it was a dam and was very big.

"Oh, thank you for telling me," replied Emily Jane, impressed at Grace's knowledge, and not wanting to show that she still had no idea which country she was in! She thought maybe she would ask her teacher when she went home. Then another thought struck her. "Suppose I am here forever and ever and never get home!" That thought frightened her!

"Look, look, be careful!" called out Grace, suddenly, in a very frightened voice. Just in front of them, in the water, was an enormous crocodile! Only its head was poking out of the water, but it was a very big head and Emily Jane could see yellow patches under its throat and massive teeth inside its mouth as it opened it. Then she realised that there were other crocodiles around the one in the water, and she shivered in fear. In fact, there were a lot of them beside the lake, blending in so well with all the surrounding water and grass that she hadn't noticed them before!

Grace took Emily Jane's hand and led her quickly away from the edge of the lake to a safer place. "My father is a fisherman, but it is so hard for him," explained Grace. "He only has half of one of his legs now. One day he was fishing in his canoe with a friend. Suddenly some hippos came very near them, and upset the canoes and they were thrown into the water. Then they were attacked by crocodiles. My father had his leg bitten. His friend was very brave and managed to pull him away, but he still lost part of his leg. We had so little money and needed to spend all we had to take him to the hospital and have treatment. He was there for such a long time. If we had had more money maybe he would have recovered faster, but we could only pay for a few medicines. Now he has a wooden part for his leg and cannot walk well. He still tries to fish so we have food, but we are all scared of the crocodiles."

Emily Jane was horrified by this tale and didn't know what to say, so she just nodded. Grace smiled though. "I'm so glad my dad is still alive! God is so good to us and helps us with everything. I go to school, I have a dress, and I eat a meal most days; we say thank you to God every day for looking after us!"

For a while Emily Jane was very quiet. She thought how angry she was that her dad had been hurt in an accident and that she couldn't have all the latest fashionable clothes and a mobile phone, because he couldn't go to work now. She felt ashamed, too, because when she prayed she didn't feel like thanking God for anything, only asking him to give her things like the high-heeled boots she wanted.

"My dad, too, was injured in an accident," Emily Jane told Grace quietly. "He now has to be pushed around in a wheelchair, and can't go to work."

"You must be very glad that he is alive, and that you have such a chair with wheels for him. Do you have money for food, since he cannot work? I am so glad that you have such a nice pair of jeans and such a pretty top to wear. And your shoes are the nicest I have ever, ever seen!"

"Where I come from the government give us some help for our rent, food and things like that. We don't have to pay for the doctor or hospital either. And everyone goes to school because it is free."

Grace opened her mouth and stared in amazement. "What a wonderful place you live in; it sounds to me like heaven!" Emily Jane laughed at that. It certainly wasn't heaven where she lived, with dirty streets and high-rise blocks of flats. She thought that Jinja seemed more like heaven with the sunshine and trees and beautiful lake, even though it did have crocodiles! Still, Emily Jane could see what Grace meant.

The two girls walked up to one of the small mud houses. The door was open, but it looked quite dark inside. "There is no electricity in this house," thought Emily Jane. Outside the house, in one of the tiny huts, she could see a lady stirring a large pottery cooking pot over an open fire. "I guessed right," Emily Jane said to herself, "the hut is the kitchen!" The smell of cooking made her feel hungry.

"This is where I live," said Grace. "Please come in,

Jane, and meet my family." Grace took off her flip flops and left them neatly outside the door. Emily Jane bent down to take off her shoes as well, copying what Grace had done.

As soon as she had taken off her shoes, Emily Jane realised that she was back in her own room, lying on her bed. There was her desk with her new watercolour pencils and drawing of the flower garden, just as she had left them. She looked at her books on the shelf, and wondered if Grace had any books. The sun was now shining through the window. Emily Jane was glad she had glass in her window! How pretty the curtains looked with their multi-coloured stripes! It was as if she had never really looked at them before. How beautiful her room was compared to Grace's mud hut!

Had she been dreaming? It had all seemed so real! She looked at her shiny shoes, and somehow they didn't seem quite so horrible. She smiled at them, and spoke to them. "I don't know if I just fell asleep and had a dream, but I like you a little better now!" Carefully she put them back into the box and lifted it on to the shelf.

THREE

The Start of a Project

Emily Jane heard her mother calling her to come down for her dinner. Surely it couldn't be that time already! She must have gone to sleep! Even so, the "dream" wouldn't go away. In her imagination Emily Jane was able to see Grace, Lake Victoria, the crocodiles and the little mud house very clearly. She had had such a lovely time in Africa, whether it was a dream or not!

She went downstairs and her mum was relieved to see that Emily Jane's bad temper face had gone and her daughter seemed happy again. They went to the table, and Dad was just about to say grace to thank God for the food when Emily Jane suddenly asked if she could say it.

"Why, of course, dear," said her father, who was very surprised as she had never asked to do that before.

"Thank you, Father God, very much that we have lots of food every day. I'm very sorry that some people in Africa don't have much to eat. Please don't let them be hungry any more. Amen."

"That was a lovely prayer," said her mum. "What made you want to say grace today?"

"I can't really explain," replied Emily Jane. She wasn't going to tell anyone about her "dream", at least not yet, not until she had thought about it more. But she couldn't forget Grace, who looked so poor and so thin, and yet who thanked God for everything.

The next day, being Sunday, Emily Jane went to church with her parents. When she was getting ready her mum suggested she put on her new shoes, but there was no way Emily Jane was going to be seen in public in those! Her mum might like them, and for that matter, so might Grace, who she now thought of as her African friend, but she still did not have to like them herself! She put on her old trainers, and couldn't help wishing "If only . . . !", then she remembered and quietly said, "Thank you, God, that I have shoes on my feet, even if they are not the ones I want."

After the worship in church, Emily Jane went to join her Sunday School group. She enjoyed the stories her teacher told, and the activities they did afterwards. That day, the story was about baby Moses. She listened as she heard how he was put into a basket when he was only three months old, and placed into the River Nile. Suddenly she remembered something that Grace had said about Jinja being where the River Nile began! She thought about the crocodiles beside the river – surely they would have eaten baby Moses, if God had not protected him! She excitedly told her group that the River Nile began at a place called Jinja, flowing out of a lake called Victoria, and there were so many huge crocodiles that it was a miracle that Moses wasn't eaten!

Her teacher looked at her in surprise. "Well, Emily Jane, anyone would think that you had actually *been* to Uganda and seen the crocodiles yourself to hear you talk! I suppose it was a miracle that Moses wasn't eaten by crocodiles, I had never thought about that before. How did you know about the source of the Nile?"

Emily Jane blushed a bit and went quiet. "I just heard it once," she said, still not wanting to share her secret "dream" just yet, but now she knew where Jinja was; it was in Uganda! She had been to Uganda! She had a friend in Uganda! Suddenly she wondered where Auntie Lucy lived. Was that Uganda too?

On the way home from church, Emily Jane asked her parents.

"In Africa, dear," her mother answered.

"I know, but where in Africa? Is it Uganda?"

"No, dear, why do you ask? What do you know about Uganda?"

"Oh, nothing much, just that the River Nile starts there and we talked about that at Sunday School," she answered, not wanting her mother to ask too many questions. "So where *does* Auntie live?"

"In a small country on the west side of Africa, called The Gambia. It is called that because it also has a big river called the River Gambia."

"If you like," said Dad, "we can get out the atlas when

we get home and look at these places."

"Yes please," answered Emily Jane, "I really want to see where Uganda is on the map. Oh, and by the way, are there crocodiles in the River Gambia?"

"Well, I don't really know, but your new shoes were made there, by someone who knows what crocodile skin looks like," answered her mum, "so I expect there are."

After dinner, Dad asked Mum to get the atlas down from the bookshelf. It was very big and heavy, so Dad and Emily Jane sat at the table. They found the map of Africa and looked at Uganda and The Gambia together. Emily Jane was amazed to see how far apart they were!

On Monday, she couldn't wait to get to school. She wanted to find out more about crocodiles, the River Nile and Africa! She thought she might tell her friend Jenna about her adventure, but then she decided not to; Jenna would probably think she was just making up stories and make fun of her.

When she had a chance, Emily Jane asked her teacher if she could look up crocodiles on the Internet. Mrs Brown was pleased that she wanted to find something out for herself, and suggested that she might like to do her new project about crocodiles. Most of the children had already started their projects, but Emily Jane had had trouble deciding what she wanted to do hers on. She was quiet for a moment, thinking about it. She didn't want anyone to learn about her "dream" but she did want to learn more about Africa and crocodiles.

"All right, Mrs Brown," she replied to her teacher, "but it might take me a long time because our Internet's not working at the moment."

"Don't worry, you can use the computers here and I will help you. It should be good fun!"

So they began. One thing Emily Jane was amazed to find out was that some crocodiles were so big they weighed as much as 1,200kg! They could eat large animals, but having had a good meal they sometimes waited for a whole year before they ate again. A whole year! She found that very hard to take in. How could any animal wait so long? It must become very hungry!

"There are very large crocodiles in Lake Victoria in Uganda. The River Nile starts there," Emily Jane told her teacher.

"That's absolutely right," said Mrs Brown. "Why don't you draw a picture at home to go in your folder about crocodiles?"

"Oh yes, I can do that!" answered Emily Jane with a smile. "I had some watercolour pencils from Grandma and Granddad for my birthday. I could do a really good picture with those! It could be the cover."

When school was over she ran to her mum who had come to meet her. "I am going to do a picture this evening," she announced. "We have to start a new project at school, and I've decided to do mine on crocodiles."

In fact, she drew a very good picture, just as she had seen the crocodiles beside Lake Victoria, with the fish drying and Grace next to some small houses. She showed her mum, who was very puzzled because it seemed almost as if Emily Jane had been there!

After tea Emily Jane looked at her picture again and took it into her bedroom. It made her think of her birthday shoes. She took them out of their box and stroked them. They did look very much like the skin of a crocodile. Perhaps she would just try them on again! She put one shoe on, then the other.

FOUR

The Secret in the Sand

Wherever was she now? Emily Jane looked around her. She was looking to see if she was back in Uganda. It didn't seem like the same place, yet it was just as warm and sunny, with a bright blue sky. She turned slowly around and all she could see were hills in the distance. They seemed a greeny-blue hazy colour. As she looked, she could see orange lines snaking up the hills; they must be paths between the trees! Everywhere, too, she could see what looked like brown boxes, which she decided must be houses. She felt excited inside, and was sure she must be back in Africa.

What was she to do now? Where should she go? The ground on which she was standing was dry with small bushes and short, but spiky grass. It seemed to be in the middle of nowhere! Emily Jane was just thinking about this when she heard a noise close to her. She looked around to find out what had made the noise, feeling a little bit scared in case it was a wild animal. What she saw was a small black and brown goat, tied to a bush by a piece of string.

"Oh you poor thing," she said. "Who has tied you up like that! Here, let me untie you!" She was just reaching out to undo the knot when she heard a shout.

"Oya!" Startled, she jumped away from the little goat, and saw a boy about her age, holding a stick and looking quite cross. Emily Jane was scared for a moment that the boy might hit her with the stick.

She thought perhaps "oya" might be some sort of greeting, so she called "oya" back, trying to sound friendly. Suddenly the little boy laughed, and though she didn't know why, she began to laugh, too. They stood and laughed for a while, then the boy began to speak to her. She couldn't understand his language at first, but then it was as if a voice was telling her what he was saying, and when she spoke back to the boy, it seemed he understood her words, too. It was very weird, like a fairy magic. "Oya means no," explained the boy. "I wanted you to stop untying my goat!"

He told her that his name was Claude, and that he was 11 years old. He spent most days looking after the family goats.

"Don't you go to school?" asked Emily Jane.

"When there is money for exercise books and pencils, and for my uniform, I can go. I like school and really wish I could always go, but there are many children in our family and we take it in turns."

"I am the only child in my family," Emily Jane told him. "I wish I had brothers and sisters, but my dad had an accident and so Mum told me that as he cannot earn money, it is best there is only me."

"I have no father now," replied Claude. "He was a soldier and died fighting the rebel soldiers. He was a hero. It is very hard for my mother now. I am the eldest son. I have four younger brothers and sisters. When I am grown up I will look after my mother. That is why I really want to attend school, so that I can get a good job and earn good money. We miss our father very much. It was just over a year ago that he died. My mother was pregnant at the time with Samson, our youngest brother. When he was born she called him Samson, hoping he would be strong, but he is often weak and sick. Mother needs me to help her look after the goats and grow vegetables. So that's another reason why I can not often go to school."

Emily Jane thought about her school. She had never even thought about whether she wanted to go or not. She just went because that is what happened when you got to be four or five. At school there was plenty of paper and pencils and many other things as well. Her mum was even given extra money to help to buy her uniform since her dad was disabled. She had taken it all for granted.

"Where are you going?" asked Claude. "What are you doing here?"

"I don't know, I am just here," she replied. Claude didn't seem to think there was anything odd about this, so proceeded to tell her that he had a secret at the lakeside. This sounded exciting. Emily Jane loved secrets!

"Tell me what it is!"

"Come with me and I will show you. Are you wearing shoes?" Claude looked down at her feet and gasped as he saw her shiny bar shoes. "Those are very special shoes," he commented. "Walk carefully so that you don't spoil them!" Emily Jane looked at Claude's feet and saw he had rubber flip flops that were looking very old.

"We need to wear shoes if you are coming with me to see my secret," he added, "because the path is stony. First we'll take this little goat back to the house."

He untied the goat and Emily Jane followed as Claude made his way along a small, dusty path to a little house that was made of mud, and was very dark inside. It reminded her of the house where Grace lived. He pushed the goat inside and pulled the corrugated iron door closed. "Now, come with me," he said, excitement in his voice.

Claude led the way down the hill. It was really quite steep, but also good fun to run down. It was a long way, and as they turned the last corner, Emily Jane was amazed to see a beautiful lake in front of her. Beyond the lake were yet more hills, stretching away into the distance. She stopped to look, her eyes filled with wonder.

"Over there, the other side of the lake, is Burundi," said Claude. "Once it was all part of Rwanda; we were the same country. Our people are very alike and we speak almost the same language. However, we are proud to be Rwandan, and I guess the Burundians feel the same about their land! My father fought for freedom in our land," Claude added proudly.

Now she knew where she was – Rwanda! Emily Jane tried to remember the map of Africa that she had looked at with her dad. Try as she might, she couldn't remember seeing Rwanda on the map. When she got home, if she got home, she would look on the map. Suddenly a feeling of panic and fear went through her. "What if I never go home?" She frowned as she tried to think how she had got home from Uganda, but she couldn't remember. Exciting though it was to be on an adventure, she knew she wanted to go home at the end of it and be back with her parents again!

"Come on," called Claude, breaking into her thoughts, "we are almost there!"

Emily Jane pushed her thoughts away because she was enjoying her adventure and wanted to see the secret, so she followed Claude.

"Come very quietly," Claude whispered. "We are near the water's edge and do not want to make the crocodiles frightened and angry. Let me go first and make sure there is no crocodile near my secret." Emily Jane's heart thumped as she waited for Claude to give the all-clear.

After a minute, Claude signalled to her that it was safe to come near. He was standing on a sandy shore by a mound of sand, which he began to scrape gently away.

"This is a crocodile nest!" he told her, his eyes shining. "I found it myself! It has eight eggs. I think they will hatch soon. Isn't that amazing!"

Emily Jane looked at the shiny white eggs in the sand and could see under the shell there was a creature growing. She was fascinated.

"I didn't know crocodiles laid eggs and had nests," she said, peering closer. Suddenly one began to crack. Emily Jane gasped in surprise as out came a tiny, slimy little creature – it was a perfect, tiny crocodile, just a few centimetres long! It looked so sweet, she just couldn't imagine it growing up into a horrible big creature that might bite the limbs of humans, or kill and eat an antelope when it came to drink.

Within a short time several small crocodiles had hatched. It was such fun watching them! But then a sort of hissing, huffing sound came from the lake.

"Run away from the lake and up the path quickly!" said Claude. "The mother crocodile has come for her babies; she mustn't find us here!" Emily Jane didn't need to be told twice!

They ran to a safe place and watched as the mother crocodile put her babies in her strong jaws and carried them gently in her mouth into the lake.

"That was a lucky escape!" said Emily Jane, thinking of Grace's daddy. "Is it OK to stop here – is it safe?"

"Yes. The crocodile will not come up here. She is a good mother and is helping her babies. Well, you came just at the right time! The only thing that might bother us here are ants. Sometimes they are fierce and sting."

Claude sat down and kicked off his flip flops. Emily Jane was hot, so she undid her shoes and kicked them off, too, and suddenly, there she was, back in her own bedroom.

She sat still for a while and thought about what had happened. Were her shoes magic? They must be, she decided. Could she have adventures whenever she wanted, just by putting on her shoes? She had worked out that she could come home again when she took them off. All the boots in the world seemed a bit tame compared with magic shoes! She decided that they would have to be a secret. She still did not want to wear her shoes to school or anywhere else, she would just keep them and her secret to herself.

Then she thought about Claude, and how much he wanted to go to school each day, and how she had never thought once to be grateful for her school. She thought about all the equipment they had, too – not just books and pencils and pens, but musical instruments and PE equipment, a large playing field, balls and netball hoops, computers and her kind teacher. Sometimes she felt very disgruntled because she didn't have her own computer, or for that matter a television in her bedroom like so many of her friends, but she had so many advantages, so many things that Claude had to do without. Yet he had seemed so happy and had shared his wonderful secret with her, and she had seen the baby crocodiles hatch. For so long Emily Jane had felt angry with God, who had not saved her father from being hurt in the accident. Claude didn't even have a father to take care of him at all.

Emily Jane wasn't usually very good when it came to praying. Mostly she had thought it was a bit of a waste of time and she was not sure that God even heard her anyway. Now she knelt down by her bed. It seemed the right thing to do, somehow. She meant it from her heart when she prayed, "Dear God, I am sorry that I grumble so much. Please help me to be different. And, thank you for my dad, thank you that he didn't die, like Claude's dad." Suddenly she was really, really glad that her dad wasn't dead. She ran down to the living room and flung herself into her father's lap, and gave him a big hug.

"Steady on, my little princess, you'll knock me out of my chair," laughed her dad. "What is all this about?"

"I just want to tell you I love you so very much and I am so glad that you are still alive!" she answered.

"I love, you, too, Princess," he answered, giving her a big kiss, before she ran into the kitchen to tell her mum she loved her, too. Her father smiled, wondering what was happening to his daughter. Something was changing her from a sulky, discontented person into this more thoughtful and loving one. Whatever it was, he was very glad!

FIVE

Good News

Once again, Emily Jane couldn't wait to get to school. She had drawn and painted another good picture of the crocodile eggs and the tiny crocodiles hatching from the nest, and she wanted to show her teacher. She had to be patient while they did the morning lessons, but just before lunch Mrs Brown came over to her table and asked her how she was getting on with her project. Mrs Brown was so pleased to see Emily Jane doing so well – she had almost despaired of getting her to do anything!

"Just see my picture!" said Emily Jane. "Did you know that crocodiles have nests, made of sand, and they lay white eggs in them and cover them with sand to protect them, then when they hatch out the mother crocodile puts them gently in her mouth and takes them down to the water!"

Emily Jane was quite breathless when she said all this, because she so much wanted to tell Mrs Brown about what she had seen.

Mrs Brown was astonished. Emily Jane had never shown so much interest in a project before, and she seemed to be learning so much. "How did you find out about this?" she asked. Emily Jane paused for a moment. How much should she tell Mrs Brown? She knew she wouldn't believe her if she told her about the birthday shoes, but she did not want to tell lies, either.

"Well," she answered, "I have a friend who lives in Rwanda, called Claude. The eggs were his secret and he told me about them. He found them in the nest on the shore of a lake near his village. The other side of the lake is another country called Burundi."

Mrs Brown didn't quite know what to think. Emily Jane was clearly telling her the truth, but it did seem strange. If she had said she had a friend in Jamaica it would have been more understandable. Anyway, she told her to put the picture in her folder and try to write about the eggs. She also said to Emily Jane that since her work was so good, if she kept it up she might get a merit award.

Wow! That pleased Emily Jane. She had never earned a merit award in all her time at school. You had to do something very special to earn one. Wouldn't her parents be pleased with her! This was her last year at primary school and at last she would have earned a merit! Up until now the only thing she had been good at had been art and games, especially netball. Lessons had never seemed very interesting before!

When school was over she went to the cloakroom to get her coat, ready to go home, and Mrs Brown came over to her. "Emily Jane," she said, "your parents have just telephoned. Your father is at the hospital having a check up and they have been held up. They have asked you to go home with Jenna and they will fetch you later. It's all arranged with Jenna's mum."

"OK, thank you, Mrs Brown," she said, and ran off to the school gates where she could see Jenna and her mother waiting for her. It would be good fun to go out to tea for a change!

Jenna was so pleased to have Emily Jane for a surprise visit and they had lots of fun playing hopscotch outside the flats, then, when they became bored with that they sat on the doorstep and talked together.

"Mrs Brown seems excited about your project. Why are you doing it about crocodiles?" Jenna asked.

"I got interested after my Auntie Lucy sent me shoes for my birthday," Emily Jane explained. "Mum said the scales on them looked like crocodile skin, so I think of them as crocodile shoes, though they aren't really, they're fake."

"Oh, yes, I forgot you had shoes for your birthday. Have you ever worn them? You really wanted boots like mine, didn't you?" For a few moments Emily Jane felt a pang of jealousy as she thought of Jenna's very trendy boots. She looked so tall when she wore them because they had high heels.

"I still do want some very much," replied Emily Jane with a sigh, "but now I think my shiny shoes are quite nice. They feel nice when I touch them. I was cross to start with when I had them, but now I know that I am lucky to have shoes, because children in Africa often don't have any at all."

"Really? How can they walk outside without shoes?"

"I guess their feet must get hard and used to it," replied Emily Jane. Just then the girls heard Jenna's mother calling them for tea. It was fish fingers and chips, one of Emily Jane's favourites! Soon after tea there was a knock at the door – it was Emily Jane's mum, come to take her home. She looked very excited, thought Emily Jane. She expected her to look tired, like she usually did after her dad's appointments, especially when they had to wait an extra long time to see the doctor.

On the way home they talked about what Emily Jane had done at Jenna's, but as soon as they got back home her mum said to her, "Come and sit with us. Dad and I want to talk with you for a minute." Mystified, Emily Jane sat down next to her mum on the settee.

Dad shifted in his wheelchair. "For so long now I have sat in this chair," he said. "The physiotherapists at the hospital have tried to help me to keep fit, just in case one day I might get some feeling back in my legs. Nobody has really expected it to happen, but Mum and I have never given up hope and always asked Jesus to heal me." Emily Jane felt a tingle of excitement flood through her from the top of her head to the toes in her feet! Could it ever be possible? Did Jesus really make people better today, like he did in the Bible stories?

"The past few days I have felt just a few tingles and pins and needles in my feet," continued her father. "At first I thought it was all my imagination, but then, as I have felt this for a few days, I began to have a hope, that perhaps, just perhaps, one day our dear Lord Jesus would heal me."

Emily Jane looked from her mother to her father and saw how excited they both were. They were looking at each other and smiling that special sort of smile that tells you a lot of love is passing between them.

"So," continued Dad with a grin, "as we had an appointment to see the doctor at the hospital today anyway, we decided not to tell anyone, just to wait and talk to him. That's why we have been such a long time at the clinic. When we told him about my feeling pins and needles, he wanted to do a thorough examination. He found that I do have feeling in both legs! It means that the spinal cord was not completely severed in the car crash, and over the years it has been growing very slowly and healing itself."

"Even the doctor was amazed and said it was a miracle!" added Mum. "We told him yes, we knew it was, and we had never given up hope that Jesus would heal your dad!"

It was hard for Emily Jane to take in this wonderful news! She had almost forgotten what it was like to have a father who could walk and play ball with her and go to work. "I am so, so, so pleased!" she shouted, then after doing a little dance, ran to her dad and gave him a hug.

"Are you going to get out of your chair and walk, like the man at the temple gate did in the Bible?" she asked. "Can you do it now?"

"No, we will have to be patient. I will go every day to the hospital for treatment to help my legs to get strong and to learn to walk again. I will work as hard as I can, and walk as soon as I can, but it will probably take quite a long time," explained her father.

"Why can't it happen at once?" asked Emily Jane, "It did in the Bible!"

"In those days, there were no physiotherapists to help you. I believe the Lord Jesus has done the miracle and joined up the broken nerves, but now it is my turn to trust him and show I believe him by working very hard. Also, think how many other disabled people I will meet each time I go to the hospital! I will be able to encourage them and tell them that Jesus is alive and still makes people well, even today!"

"I want you to walk *now*, but I, too, will ask Jesus to help me to be patient and wait for the miracle to be finished. But is it all right to tell Jenna and Mrs Brown, my teacher?"

"Yes, now that the doctor has confirmed what is happening, of course you can," replied her dad. "Now, shall we say a 'thank you' prayer to the Lord Jesus before you go to bed?"

Emily Jane once again felt this was a special time and so she knelt down beside her father and buried her face in his lap. Her father said a prayer, thanking Jesus for this wonderful miracle. Emily Jane said a loud "Amen," but then felt this was just not enough, she needed to add her own prayer.

"Lord Jesus, I love my dad so much. I was very angry when you let him be so hurt. I am sorry about that. I am so glad he didn't die and now you are making him well just like the man in the Bible. I can't wait to see him walk again! Help me to be good and patient. Amen."

SIX

Sharing the Secret

Emily Jane was hopping from one foot to another, "Come *on*!" she called to her mum, "I want to get to school *now*!" She couldn't wait to share the good news about her dad with her teacher and her best friend. She thought that now that she was 11 she should be allowed to walk to school on her own, but the area where they lived had a lot of problems and the headmaster liked all the pupils to be accompanied to and from school.

"Now," answered her mother, "who prayed last night to be patient? We are all going to have to learn to be patient, and it won't be easy for any of us, either!"

"Sorry, Mum, I forgot," answered Emily Jane, but it wasn't very long before they were out of the door and going up the hill to the school. Emily Jane tried not to run all the way, but it was hard not to!

She gave her mum a hug and ran into the classroom. Mrs Brown was at her desk getting the register ready. She looked up when she saw Emily Jane running through the classroom.

"Whatever is it, Emily Jane? You know you are not

allowed to run in the classroom! Calm down! You look very pleased with yourself. Have you found out more facts about crocodiles?"

"I have much more exciting news than that!" Emily Jane's words were just tumbling out one after another. She was dancing up and down from one foot to the other! "Guess what? The best news ever! My dad is going to walk again!"

Mrs Brown could hardly believe her ears. "That sounds the best news I have heard in a very long time!" she said with a big smile. "Would you like to come with me and we will find a quiet place, so that you can tell me all about it?"

Mrs Brown asked the classroom assistant to help everyone come in and settle while she took Emily Jane to a quiet corner. "Now, tell me everything," she said. A breathless Emily Jane tried to tell her teacher all her parents had told her last night, even telling her that it was a miracle like the Bible story.

"You know," said her teacher, "this is such special news, I think we should tell the whole school in assembly, and we can all say a prayer for your father. Would you like to tell everyone, or shall I?"

"I don't mind doing it, if you stand with me to help me," replied Emily Jane, "but first, can I tell Jenna, because she is my best friend?"

"That's a very good idea," said Mrs Brown, nodding. "Now we will go and ask the headmaster, I'm sure he will agree." They walked along the corridor to his office and knocked at the door.

"Come in!" he called. They went in together, and he looked at Emily Jane.

"What have you been up to, young lady?" he asked, thinking she must have misbehaved.

"Nothing, sir," replied Emily Jane with a beaming smile. "I've got some good news!"

Mrs Brown went on to explain about Emily Jane's dad, and the headmaster thought it was an excellent idea to share the good news with the whole school at assembly. When the accident had happened, they had shared the news at assembly and prayed for the whole family. Now they could all be glad that their prayers had worked!

When Emily Jane got back to the classroom, she was smiling so widely that Jenna wondered what was up, and quickly looked at her friend's feet, wondering if maybe she had got the boots she wanted so much. However, she was wearing her old shoes as usual!

"What's up, Em?" she whispered.

"Tell you later," Emily Jane whispered back.

At playtime Jenna couldn't wait to hear what had happened.

"Come on, Em," she said, "spill the beans! You have been grinning like the Cheshire cat from *Alice in Wonderland* all morning!"

They went over to the grass and sat at a picnic bench. Emily Jane told her the wonderful news, and Jenna was so pleased for her friend. "Please keep my secret until assembly," Emily Jane asked. "We are going to tell the whole school then."

Assembly was just before lunch. Emily Jane started to get butterflies when it was her turn to go on the stage and tell everyone about her dad. Then she remembered how brave he was and that made her want to be brave like him. She told everyone that they had to be patient and her dad would have to work very hard every day, but one day he would walk again, properly, like the man in the Bible, because Jesus could still make people well.

Everyone clapped and cheered. Many of them had seen Emily Jane's father in his wheelchair, and were thrilled to hear such good news.

Then the headmaster reminded everyone that they had prayed after the accident. "Now," he explained, "we have to all say thank you that one day Mr Peters will walk again. And we will ask God to go on making his legs strong enough to walk."

The school became very quiet. After the prayer everyone clapped and cheered again before they went for their lunch break. Mrs Brown came over to Emily Jane and told her she had managed very well, and she was proud of her.

Mum had pushed her dad up the hill to meet Emily Jane from school as she sometimes did and soon there were many children and parents around them, saying how pleased they were at the good news.

"You were a very brave girl to stand up on the stage and tell the school our good news," her father said, when he heard what Emily Jane had done.

"I was scared at first, and then I remembered what you had said about telling the other disabled people that Jesus can still make people well. Then I wanted to do the same," Emily Jane replied.

Her dad smiled and said, "That's why Auntie Lucy went to live in Africa; so she could talk to people who didn't already know that Jesus cares about them and answers our prayers." Well, that was quite a new thought to Emily Jane! "I wouldn't mind living in Africa," she thought to herself. "All I know about Africa is very interesting, except for the horrible big crocodiles!" That made her wonder how the baby crocodiles were doing, and how Claude was.

SEVEN

Back in Rwanda

As soon as she got home, Emily Jane rushed up to her room and shut the door. She really wanted to see if she could go to Africa every time she put on her birthday shoes. She took them out of the box and stroked them, feeling the scales that were pretend crocodile skin. "Mum was right," she thought. "The person who made this shiny leather must know what crocodiles look like, it looks so real." She had to admit that the patterns looked quite beautiful. That gave her an idea. Emily Jane took a piece of white paper and gently rubbed over the pattern with a brown wax crayon. The impression turned out really well and she put it in her project folder. Another interesting piece of work to show Mrs Brown!

Then Emily Jane sat on her bed and took off her slippers. First she put on the right shoe, and paused for a few seconds before putting on the other one, feeling slightly nervous. Would the shoes take her to Africa again this time? Would she be back with Grace, or Claude, or somewhere completely different? Just as before, when she slipped on the second shoe she felt her eyes becoming very heavy as if she were slipping into another world. When she opened her eyes she looked around to see if she could recognise where she was standing. To her delight Claude was running towards her, looking pleased to see her! Emily Jane ran to meet her new friend. She looked round at the bluey-green hills all around her and breathed deeply to fill her lungs with the warm air. It was such a change after the winter at home!

"I am so glad you have come again!" said Claude with a grin. "I was just going to the lake to see the crocodiles. Do you want to come with me?" Claude helped her scramble down the path to the lake shore. The crocodile nest was still there, with just two eggs remaining that had not hatched.

"Sometimes they are sterile, which means they haven't got a baby crocodile in them," explained Claude. He carefully picked up one egg and held it up to the sun. "This one has a baby in it, look, you can see it!" he exclaimed. "It must be almost ready to hatch." Emily Jane carefully picked up the second egg and copied what Claude had done. She held it up to the sun's rays, but was very disappointed as she saw no baby crocodile inside.

"That is a dud one," Claude told her. "There is almost always one in the clutch that is no good. Leave it on the shore and some animal will find it for food."

As they were talking, the shell of the other egg began to crack and they saw the tiny crocodile force its way out. It lay in the sun to let the sticky layer dry out. The children moved back from the shore, as they expected the mother to come and collect it, just as she had done with her other babies. They were so busy watching for her in the water that they did not see a bird approach from above; in seconds a heron had swooped down and taken the tiny crocodile! "Oh my goodness!" gasped Emily Jane in shock, watching the big bird fly away.

"Oh dear," moaned Claude, "that is always a problem when the crocodiles are so tiny. Fish eagles and herons and black kites swoop down and steal them. That is why the mother has to protect them in her mouth."

It was beautiful by the lake; a slight breeze kept them from being too hot and it was wonderful to watch the water ripple at the edges. As they stayed there, they saw the mother crocodile swimming by. Near her were the other baby crocodiles, growing fast!

"Thank goodness they are all right," said Emily Jane.

"I thought you hated crocodiles!" laughed Claude.

"Well I do, but the babies are so cute and funny, I want them to survive!"

"Shall we go out in a canoe for a while?" asked Claude. "We can see lots more interesting things out on the lake." For a few moments Emily Jane hesitated. She remembered Grace in Uganda and how her father had been hurt while fishing. Would she be safe? She looked at Claude and he looked so confident that she decided to go with him. She could always take off her shoes and get home in an emergency!

"Yes, I'd like to come. Thank you," she replied, smiling. Claude grinned back. It was good to have friends!

Claude led the way around the shore of the lake, being very careful to look and see if any crocodiles were basking in the sun near the path. He did not want to surprise and anger one! He told Emily Jane that they had such cold blood that they needed to sunbathe to keep warm and save energy. If they were frightened or suddenly disturbed as they walked past, the crocodiles could be dangerous. Emily Jane stored up all this information in her memory so that she could include it in her school project. She had no idea that homework and school work could be such fun!

"Tell me more about your school, Claude," she asked.

"Well, mine is only a small village school, with about 800 children."

"Eight hundred?" Emily Jane almost screamed at him. "You call that small? It is huge!"

Claude grinned. "We have about 50 to 60 children in each class. Some of us go in the morning and others after lunch. There are not enough classrooms for us all at the moment, so my class has to sit outside under a large mango tree. The blackboard is nailed to the tree trunk, and we each sit on a mud brick. It can be very hard and uncomfortable, but at least we get to learn!"

"What happens when it rains?" asked Emily Jane. "Do you still sit outside?"

"We move to the veranda that is around the classroom. It is not so good, because the rain makes such a noise on the tin roof, and also you hear the other class doing their lessons. It is cold when it rains, too, so it is hard to concentrate. The school belongs to the church and they are raising money to build us some new classrooms. I think it will take a long time. What about your school, do you always do your lessons indoors?"

Emily Jane felt embarrassed because her school was so nice! "Well, everyone has a classroom. My school is called Windy Hill Primary School. It is on a hill, but not such a big hill as the ones around here. There are 30 children in my class and we start at nine in the morning. I have my dinner at school. Some children bring a packed lunch. The dinners are quite nice, and you can choose different things. Then we have classes again until three in the afternoon. I am in year six, so next year I will go to senior school. I don't know which one it will be. We hear just before Easter. My best friend is called Jenna and we want to go to the same school if we can."

Emily Jane didn't really want to talk any more about her school, because it would sound like she was boasting if she told Claude about the computers and televisions, art materials and PE equipment. She just added, "My teacher is called Mrs Brown, and I like her very much."

"That's good," said Claude. "I really hope I can go back to school soon. I have to learn enough to pass my national examination that allows me to go into the next class. I don't suppose I will ever get to senior school, though I would love to!"

When they reached the lake shore Claude untied a dugout canoe. He helped Emily Jane climb into it, then climbed in himself and began to paddle. He was strong, even though he was only 11 years old. The canoe began to move away from the shore quite quickly. They negotiated the clumps of papyrus reeds. Emily Jane didn't know what they were and asked about the tall reeds with pompoms on the top. When Claude told her they were papyrus and they made paper from the insides of the reeds, she was astonished!

Once they were clear of the reeds they headed out to the middle of the lake. Claude pointed to some hippos as they came up out of the water to breathe, making a loud snorting sound. "We won't get too near them," he said. "They are very dangerous animals!"

Out in the lake, Claude stopped paddling and threw a large net into the water. "I want to catch some fish for my mother. It is very good protein for the family." It didn't take long before he felt the net was heavy, and the two children began to pull it in together. There were about a dozen fish inside! They looked very ugly to Emily Jane as they wriggled around, but Claude was pleased with his catch. He threw the small fish back.

"They are too small to eat. Let them grow big for another time. These big Tilapia fish taste really good! Let's get back to the shore and I will take them home while they are fresh." The fish were wriggling in the net, but could not escape.

Claude was paddling back to shore when it happened! A very large crocodile came underneath the canoe, giving it such a bump! The canoe shook and then began to turn over! Suddenly Emily Jane could feel the cold water swirling around her. She was terrified; surely they would both die – the crocodile would eat them alive! She saw the canoe, swam to it and clung on, gasping for breath. How glad she was that she was a good swimmer! Then she looked round for Claude, and she saw him nearby, but he seemed unable to move. Horrified, she noticed the crocodile was between him and the boat! Emily Jane saw the paddle floating near her and grabbed it. Without thinking, she whacked the crocodile with the paddle, not just once, but over and over again. It must have been surprised by her attack, because it swam away.

Claude swam to the canoe and somehow managed to turn it up the right way again. They both clambered in. Claude took the paddle from Emily Jane and paddled for all he was worth back to the shore. Neither child spoke. They were too shocked, and were shaking all over.

On the shore, some fishermen had seen what was happening and had run to see if they could help. They helped them out of the canoe and when they saw that they were both still alive, they clapped and applauded them for being so brave and managing to escape. Claude's arm was cut and badly bruised; he must have hurt it when the boat overturned. He was almost crying with the pain, but it didn't seem to be broken. Emily Jane had whacked the crocodile just in time! They had lost all the fish, but that was the last thing on their minds.

The fishermen wrapped each child in a *kitenge*, a length of cloth like a blanket, and carried them to Claude's auntie's hut to recover from their ordeal. It was dark and cool inside. Auntie threw up her hands in shock when she saw the children and chattered away while she made them some sweet tea and gave them a sort of pancake to eat. They were still shivering from the cold. She took Claude's shorts and T-shirt and left him wrapped in a cloth while his clothes dried in the sun, then bathed his arm gently with some warm water. Then she took off her headscarf and made it into a sling for his arm. Emily Jane saw that he was feeling better and was glad to see him drop off to sleep. Next, the lady came to help her. She undid her shoes and took them off her feet. Emily Jane thanked the kind lady as she reached out and took them in her hand. She didn't want to lose her magic shoes! Her eyes closed, and when she opened them again she was on her bed at home. Emily Jane lay on her bed still feeling shocked and a bit cold. She realised she still had her shoes in her hand. She put them down, pulled the duvet over her and fell fast asleep.

EIGHT

Jenna Tries the Shoes

Just as Emily Jane sat up, her mum came up. "Oh there you are, Emily Jane. You were so quiet that I wondered what you were up to!" she said. Then her mother saw the shiny birthday shoes. "I see you've been looking at your shoes! I thought we would telephone Auntie Lucy this evening and tell her the good news about your dad. You could talk to her too, and thank her for your present, if you like."

"Yes, please, I would like to do that," answered Emily Jane, still half-thinking about Claude and their narrow escape from the crocodile. "They are sort of very special shoes."

"Indeed," answered her mum. "Now, dear, can you come and help me by setting the table? The ambulance will soon be bringing Dad home from hospital. I wonder how he got on today?"

Emily Jane put her slippers on and ran downstairs. She was glad to help out. Sometimes her mother looked so tired and she knew it was hard work to take care of her dad. How wonderful it would be when her dad could walk again! As she put out the knives and forks for their meal, she whispered a prayer to God. "I know I can ask you anything at any time, so even though this is not in church, and I am not kneeling down or anything like that, I want to ask you to help my dad to walk soon, please. And I hope Claude's all right. Please make his arm better too. Amen."

Emily Jane wondered actually what "Amen" meant, but everyone said it when they finished a prayer, so she thought she had better add it. Maybe her dad could tell her what it meant.

Her father was tired when the ambulance brought him home, but he looked cheerful. He wheeled his chair into the lounge with a huge smile on his face. "I stood up on my feet!" he told Emily Jane and her mum, who clapped and cheered! "I had to hold on to the two bars, but I could feel my own feet tingling! It was just amazing! Now I need to sit and rest a bit. How about my little princess coming and having a chat with me?"

Emily Jane needed no second invitation. She sat on the couch as near to her dad as she was able.

"First, Dad, I want to ask you something," she said.

"Go ahead, princess, I'll do my best to answer. I hope it's not about crocodiles; you know more about them than I do, now!" he laughed.

"I want to know what 'amen' means, and why everyone says it at the end of a prayer. Do you know?"

"It means, 'So be it!' It is an old fashioned word that

says 'Yes, I agree with the prayer.' Sort of saying, 'OK God, I really mean that!'"

"Oh, that's good. I'll always say Amen when I pray then. I want my prayers to be answered."

"Sure, sweetheart, but we always have to remember that sometimes God says, 'Wait a bit longer', or 'No, that is not the best I have for you.' He does not always say, 'Yes', any more than I always say yes to all you ask me for. Sometimes we get our answers wrong, but God never does."

Her father paused for a few moments, then added, "Remember when you asked me for the boots with high heels? I had to say no, because we can't afford them. You were very disappointed, and it was hard for me to say no to you, but I knew that was what was best."

"I do understand, Dad, and I am really sorry that I sulked so much. Actually, I haven't thought about the boots very much lately. I have had so much else to think about, like crocodiles and Africa. Dad," she went on, "are you too tired to look at the atlas together again?"

"No problem, but be careful how you take it from the bookshelf. It is a very heavy book." They turned to the page which had a big map of the whole of Africa on it.

"Remember where Uganda is?" asked her dad. Emily Jane pored over the page and pointed out Uganda, and then found Lake Victoria and Jinja.

"Now, Dad," she went on, "I want to find a country called Rwanda."

"Goodness me!" said her father, "I am not exactly sure where that is. I'll teach you something. I'll show you how to look up places in the index." He showed Emily Jane how to do this, and they found where Rwanda was.

"Why, it is so small!" she exclaimed, "and look, Burundi is also so small and next to it!" She looked at the map very carefully.

"What are you looking for?" asked her father.

"A lake. There is a lake which is part of the border."

"Let me look," said Dad, "Yes, there it is! It is the small blue bubble. It is much smaller than Lake Victoria and has no name on the map, but it is there all right! How did you know it was there? I suppose it is something to do with your crocodile project?"

"Yes, sort of," replied Emily Jane. She thought of the fun she had had with Claude there, and how kind his auntie was, and somehow knew that his arm would be OK.

After tea, her mother phoned The Gambia. She told Auntie Lucy the wonderful news that one day Dad would walk again. Then it was Emily Jane's turn to speak. She said thank you for her shoes.

"Do they fit you?" asked her auntie.

"An exact fit," replied Emily Jane, "and I love them, because they are so very special, sort of magic really. It's hard to explain, but they are a wonderful present, thank you."

Emily Jane was sure she heard Auntie Lucy laugh

before saying, "I will see you at Easter, because I am coming to England for a holiday. We can talk about them then!"

"That's wonderful, I can't wait!" Emily Jane said to her auntie, smiling to herself as she handed the phone back to her mum. Maybe Auntie Lucy knew all about the shoes being magic!

The next day in school, Emily Jane wrote a paragraph about fishing in lakes in Uganda and in Rwanda where crocodiles lived, for her project. She described the dugout canoes and paddles, and how good the fish were to eat, but try as she might she just could not remember the name of the ugly fish. She only remembered that it began with a T. Mrs Brown had no idea either. She suggested they looked on the Internet together. This took a while, but in the end Mrs Brown came up with the name Tilapia.

"That's it, that's it!" cried Emily Jane excitedly.

"Emily Jane," said Mrs Brown in surprise, "you are amazing me! Where have you been getting all this knowledge?" Emily Jane just grinned. Her project file was getting quite fat now. She had found out that there were 23 species of crocodiles in the world. She had no idea there were so many! She learnt that they had prehistoric dinosaur ancestors, and they had survived in their present form since then. Each time she found out something new, she became excited. Although they were fierce, she decided they were not such horrible creatures as she had once thought. It made her respect the birthday shoes, because they had taught her so much and even though she didn't want to be seen wearing them, she began to treasure them. In fact Emily Jane wondered if they were never meant to be worn as ordinary shoes. After all, if she put them on for school every morning, she would never get there, she would spend all her time in Africa!

It did occur to Emily Jane that perhaps she should share her secret with Jenna. Jenna was her best friend, and she didn't like keeping secrets from her. Would she believe her if she told her the shoes were magic? She had a feeling that she would laugh at her and tell her to stop making up stories.

Later in the week, Jenna came round after school again. It was quite warm, so for a while they played outside, then decided to give themselves new hair styles up in Emily Jane's bedroom. This kept them amused for a long time, because Jenna loved to plait Emily Jane's curly hair into tiny plaits and Emily Jane loved to weave braids into Jenna's long, dark hair. Suddenly Jenna caught sight of the birthday shoes in their box, as the lid was not on properly. She pulled them out, then said to Emily Jane, "These really do look ugly. I don't blame you for not wearing them." Emily Jane felt quite upset, because she now liked the shoes very much. "They are not ugly, exactly, they are just different," she explained. "I think my auntie must have paid a lot of money for them."

"Can I try them on?" asked Jenna. Emily Jane didn't

know what to say. How could she begin to explain that they were magic?

"Well," said Emily Jane, hesitantly, "um . . ." Then she ran out of words, but Jenna had already taken off her trainers and was trying to push her feet into the shoes.

"They are far too small, I can't get my toes into them!" said Jenna.

"Oh," Emily Jane replied, feeling very relieved that they didn't fit! Jenna kicked off the shoes and they fell on the floor. Emily Jane picked them up and put them back into the box carefully.

"Why don't you put them on?" her friend asked her. "Let me see them on your feet."

"Not now, I don't feel like it," said Emily Jane quickly, hoping for a distraction. Fortunately at that moment she heard a car outside, and went to the window. "It's Dad – home from the hospital, I wonder how he got on today?" The girls rushed downstairs to see him.

Although he looked tired, he had a wonderful smile on his face. "Do you know, girls, I took one step on my own today! Soon I will be walking – one of these days I will be taking you both out!"

"I can't wait," said Emily Jane. "It will be the best day of my life! I keep asking God to make it come quickly, so that you will be like the man in the Bible story who went walking and leaping and praising God!"

"I don't know that story," said Jenna, "Can you tell it to me?"

Emily Jane told her the story and Jenna was amazed, especially when she heard that it was true. "I have never really prayed to God, except when we pray sometimes at school assembly," she said, "but from now on, I am going to pray that your dad will soon walk and jump like that man in the story."

"Thank you," said Emily Jane's dad. "Thank you very much, Jenna."

NINE

"Salties" and Oysters

At bedtime Emily Jane added her own prayers for her dad. She asked God to make his legs strong, and help him each day to walk more steps. Then she found herself thinking about her African friends, Grace and Claude. She didn't know if they were real or dream people, but she said a prayer for them – for Grace whose dad had a wooden leg and Claude who had no father at all. She thanked God that her dad was still alive and now getting well. Then she thanked God for her school. It sounded so much better than Claude's school. She prayed for children like him who could not go to school, or who didn't have proper classrooms or pens or pencils.

After her prayers, she felt very peaceful, but not terribly sleepy. She thought about her shoes. She had been really afraid that Jenna would go to Africa in them and leave her behind! Would the magic have worked for her, too? Emily Jane didn't know. Maybe she would put them on again, right now. She took them lovingly from the box, and put them on her bare feet.

Would it matter that she was wearing her pyjamas she

suddenly thought? She giggled, because it was too late, her eyes were heavy and the lids just closed, and she was gone!

But where had she gone? Emily Jane looked around her. She had no idea where she was. Was she in Africa again? The sun was burning and she felt hotter than she had ever felt in her life. It looked a very different place from those she had visited before. The bit of sky she could see above was cloudless and very blue. Around her were strange bushes, or were they trees? They had roots that hung down from branches, and there didn't seem to be a path. Everywhere smelt damp, the ground seemed boggy and the sound of buzzing insects filled the air. She felt hot in her pyjamas, but was glad she had trousers to protect her legs. Many insects were flying around and she didn't want to be bitten!

Emily Jane began to push her way through the branches, becoming more and more anxious as the minutes passed, because it was like being lost in a very thick maze. Suddenly she almost fell into a narrow, muddy river! Someone was in a small canoe, paddling up towards her. As she came nearer, Emily Jane could see that it was a young woman, with a baby tied to her back. The woman shouted, "This is not a very good place to walk, are you lost?"

"Well, I don't really know," answered Emily Jane. She was feeling both scared and excited. Her shoes had always taken her to interesting places on her adventures, but this was very different.

"You had better come with me," replied the woman. "Climb in carefully."

Emily Jane did as she was told, partly because she didn't know what else to do. In the canoe she was surprised to see a pile of shiny grey objects, a bit like shells. She was staring at them, wondering what they were, when the woman said to her, "I have a good crop of oysters today, haven't I?"

"Are these oysters?" asked Emily Jane, "I have never seen them before. What do you do with them?"

The young woman looked surprised. "You live in The Gambia and don't know what to do with oysters? We gather them from these mangrove swamps. They are seafood – some we sell, some we eat. And then we grind the shells and mix them with water to make a paste. This makes a plaster for the walls of our houses."

"Are these trees with all the long shoots coming from them called mangroves then?" asked Emily Jane. The woman nodded, looking surprised at such ignorance, so Emily Jane added quickly, "I don't actually live here." Then she had a bright thought, "but my Auntie Lucy does! She is a nurse here."

"Well, what is she thinking of letting you loose in the mangrove swamps! You could get horribly lost!" The baby on the back of the young woman began to cry. "Hush, Fatou, don't cry," said the mother to her child.

"Shall I hold your baby for you?" asked Emily Jane.

"Yes, that would be good," answered the young mother, untying her baby and handing her carefully over. Emily Jane thought she was the sweetest baby she had ever seen. She had soft, tightly curled hair and her two dark eyes gazed at her for a long time, then she started to smile and make happy baby noises.

"You are good with babies!" said the young woman. "You are making my Fatou happy. What is your name?"

"My real name is Emily Jane, but I don't mind if you just call me Jane."

"OK, Jane. I am Ayisha. This is my first-born child. She is six months old now."

"I think she is beautiful! Thank you for letting me cuddle her. I wish I had a baby brother or sister, but I am an only child. I don't actually live with my auntie, but with my parents. My mum looks after my dad who cannot walk because of an accident."

"I'm glad your dad is still alive after his accident," replied Ayisha. "You are very much blessed, because my husband had an accident, too, but after a while he died. We had no money for the doctor and hospital, so his wounds became infected."

"I am so sorry," said Emily Jane. She didn't know what else to say; it seemed so terrible.

"This is why I come to the swamp to find oysters. I can then get a little money for food and rent. I am glad that I live here near the River Gambia, where the water is still salty and the oysters grow."

They had reached the end of the creek by now, and Ayisha leapt out of the canoe. Then she took baby Fatou from Emily Jane, so that she could get out as well. They were near a small, round mud house with a roof made of grass. Emily Jane followed Ayisha inside. Although Ayisha took off her shoes before entering, Emily Jane knew by now that her adventure would end if she did the same, so she crept in hoping Ayisha would not mind. At first she could see nothing, then, as her eyes became accustomed to the dark, she saw some furniture. In one chair sat an old lady, who nodded and smiled at her and said something in a language Emily Jane did not recognise.

"This is my grandmother," explained Ayisha. "She says welcome to you. While I have been working, she has made some soup for our meal and asks if you would you like to stay and have some with us."

Emily Jane thought for a minute then smiled at the old lady. Soup sounded very nice! "Yes please, if that is all right," she answered. "Please say thank you to your grandmother." Ayisha handed Fatou to the old lady to look after, then called Emily Jane to follow her.

"Before we eat we need to empty the oysters from the canoe," she said. "Will you help me, Jane?"

"Of course!" answered Emily Jane. She ran at once to the canoe and helped put the oysters into a brightly woven round basket. Then the basket was tied in a cloth and Ayisha balanced it on her head and took it into the house.

Once her eyes had become accustomed to the dark again, Emily Jane could see how simple the hut was. It was really just a circular room. In the middle was a fire and the smoke drifted into the thatched roof. One side of the room had some straw mats on which a cloth was neatly folded. She guessed that was where Ayisha and her grandmother slept. On the other side were two folding wooden chairs and two round low stools, a small table, and a cupboard where some dishes were kept. The dishes were white, but made of metal, and a little chipped. The cups were made of blue plastic.

The soup was made of vegetables, ground peanuts and rice. Emily Jane was a bit nervous about trying it, but it was delicious! After they had eaten, Ayisha put Fatou on her back, the basket of oysters on her head, and they set out to walk to the market. It was still so hot! They had to walk such a long way, or at least it seemed so to Emily Jane. She looked down at herself and realised she must look very funny in her pyjamas and crocodile shoes, but nobody else around her seemed to notice. Other people on the path were also wearing strange clothes. Some other children were in trousers made of brightly coloured cloth, with tunics over them. Maybe her pyjamas weren't so out of place after all! When they reached the market, Emily Jane followed Ayisha carefully, not daring to let her out of her sight in case she got lost, but wished she could have spent longer looking at all the colourful stalls full of exotic-looking fruit and vegetables, cloth, clothes and spices.

Ayisha sold her oysters and was pleased. "We did well today! I have a good price for the oysters. Maybe we'll even be able to collect some more before evening, if you can stay to help me?"

"Sure, of course I'll help!" Emily Jane was enjoying this adventure and she and Ayisha chatted animatedly on the way home, like old friends. "Why do you have to pay to go to the hospital and get medicines?" Emily Jane asked. "At home it's free, at least I think it must be, because we never take money when we need to go to the doctor or have treatment." She knew that England had something called a National Health Service, which many people moaned about. Her dad had always said English people should not grumble, as so many people in other countries had nowhere to go for help when they were sick.

Ayisha did her best to answer the questions about paying to see the doctor. She was surprised that this child knew so little about The Gambia considering her auntie was a nurse there!

When they arrived home, Grandma was delighted with the money Ayisha had earned. They all sat and chatted for a while, drinking sweet hot tea. Then baby Fatou needed to be fed and changed. Emily Jane was so surprised because she had no nappy, just a piece of old cloth tied around her. She had always thought that all babies wore proper nappies, but when she thought about it, she realised that this must be all this poor young widow could afford.

When she had finished she handed Fatou to Emily Jane again, who cuddled and played with her, singing to her some of the nursery rhymes her mum used to sing to her when she was little.

After a while Fatou yawned and Ayisha said, "I think she will sleep now, so we will leave her with Grandmother and just have a short time collecting more oysters. Then we can eat them for supper, and that will be a treat for everyone!" She led Emily Jane out into the sunshine. They made their way to the canoe, and pushed off into the narrow neck of the river. The tide was coming in, explained Ayisha, so the water was deeper and it was easier to paddle.

"Why does the tide come in when it is a river?" asked Emily Jane.

"Because we are at the mouth of the river, very near the sea, the Atlantic Ocean," Ayisha answered. "This is where slave traders in times long ago captured our people and took them in ships to become slaves in America, never to see their homes and families ever again. It was terrible. Many men and women and boys and girls died on the way. They were treated like animals." Emily Jane was horrified to hear this story. She knew this had happened, and that was why she looked African. Her grandparents had told her how her ancestors were taken from Africa to Jamaica as slaves and made to work in the sugar plantations. It had never really meant anything to her before. Now she thought how terrible it would be for people like Ayisha to be captured and taken away in ships to be slaves in another land! Perhaps her ancestors had been taken from The Gambia! Perhaps she really belonged here, in this country.

By now they had paddled to a good spot where the branches and roots of the mangrove trees were just covered with oysters clinging to them!

"Just pick off what you can reach from the canoe," explained Ayisha. "We can take as many as we like from here. Further up the river we have to leave them because they are too small. They take two years to grow, so we leave the young ones until they are bigger."

They were busy picking when Emily Jane thought she saw a log floating near by. "Mind the canoe doesn't hit the log," she said to Ayisha.

"Oh goodness, that's not a log, it's a 'saltie', we must move quietly and quickly," Ayisha whispered back.

"Saltie, what's that?" asked Emily Jane, as Ayisha skilfully moved the dugout up the side creek as fast as she could.

"It's a salt water crocodile. We don't get many here, but they are very fierce and attack people if they are hungry or annoyed. They are the most dangerous of all crocodiles, but hunters like to try and catch them, because their bellies have the best skin for making shoes and bags for rich people. They are very sought after, even though it is now against the law."

Once they could see the crocodile had not followed

them, Ayisha slowed the canoe a little and rested because she was a bit out of breath. "It may be that saltie was a female," she explained, "because she did not follow us. If she has a nest with eggs, she will guard them and not want to move far from them."

"Is her nest of sand, like the crocodiles by the lakes?" asked Emily Jane.

"No, they make a nest of leaves and soil, near to the water, but on the land. It is a huge mound and may contain as many as 50 eggs!"

Emily Jane gasped in amazement. "Fifty eggs!"

Ayisha nodded. "They lay them in the rainy season and they take between about 65 and 100 days to hatch. The warmer the nest, the more likely the babies are to be male crocodiles, and the cooler it is, they are likely to be female. Isn't that so strange?"

"That is really interesting!" agreed Emily Jane. She was fascinated. She stored up all these facts in her mind, to include in her school project. "You know a lot about crocodiles, Ayisha!"

Ayisha was quiet for a moment. "Well, Jane, my husband knew a lot about crocodiles. He used to hunt them for their skins." She looked down at Emily Jane's shoes. "Your shoes look like crocodile leather, but they are too shiny, they are pretend. That is better. We were very poor. My husband had no way to make a living except by hunting the crocodiles illegally. He hated to kill such wonderful animals. He had great respect for them. Then one day, when he was out hunting, he trapped a female who was watching her nest, but the net broke and she escaped, and turned in anger and attacked him. That was the accident from which he never recovered."

Ayisha turned her face away because she didn't want Emily Jane to see her crying. "Fatou was born soon afterwards. She will never know her father, but I will make sure she knows how very brave he was. He did what he did, even though it was illegal, to try to look after us both."

"I am so terribly sorry," said Emily Jane, wiping tears from her eyes, too. "I wonder why people want handbags and shoes made of real crocodile skin. It's horrible and dangerous. If people had shoes made to look like skin, like mine are, everything would be OK."

"You're right. Take care of those shoes you are wearing. Show people you can have smart shoes without killing crocodiles," agreed Ayisha.

Emily Jane felt ashamed when she thought of how she had hated and despised the shoes on her birthday, and how angry she was that they had been given to her instead of high-heeled boots.

"I will take care of them, and tell people it is wrong to kill crocodiles for their skin," she promised.

They paddled up the creek and pulled the canoe up to the house together. Grandmother smiled in delight when she saw the oysters. Emily Jane was given Fatou to hold again while Ayisha put some water in a bowl to give her a wash. She only had a small bowl with water poured from a plastic can.

"How hard Ayisha's life is," thought Emily Jane, as she cooed at the baby. "They just have a bowl to wash in. I'm never going to grumble again when Mum tells me to have a bath." Just then Fatou gave Emily Jane a beautiful smile, as if she understood!

Emily Jane smiled too. "Thank you for asking me to your home and for teaching me so much," she said to Ayisha.

"It's a very poor home, I'm afraid. Almost no one lives in traditional round mud houses like this one any more, but it is all we can afford," answered Ayisha.

It made Emily Jane wonder if her ancestors had lived in a hut like this one. She looked at the whitewashed walls, and marvelled that the plaster to do this had been made from the shells of oysters ground to a powder and mixed with water. Suddenly she felt tired. She yawned and stretched and without thinking, bent down and took off her shoes.

Emily Jane's bedroom door creaked open and her mother crept in. "Look at her, on top of her bed, in her pyjamas, holding her birthday shoes!" She covered her daughter with a blanket and gently kissed her forehead.

"Sweet dreams," she whispered.

TEN

Emily Jane Shares her Secret

Mrs Brown often asked Emily Jane, "How is your father getting on?" The whole class were excited when they heard he had been able to take first one step, then several. Mrs Brown suggested that they made a special big card, to congratulate and also to encourage him. Each child drew their own face on the card, then put their name and a message on it.

Jenna had written, "You are a miracle, like the man in the Bible!" as she had not forgotten the story Emily Jane had told her.

Mrs Brown asked Jenna to explain her message, so Jenna told the whole class the story, with a bit of prompting from Emily Jane from time to time. At the end, Emily Jane felt very bold and said, "Miracles are for today, not just in the Bible, because Jesus is still alive!" She went on to say, "Even the consultant at the hospital said he doesn't understand my dad's case, and that he is a living miracle!"

"That's fantastic," said Mrs Brown. "We must all continue to pray for Emily Jane's father, that he will continue to get strong."

Later that morning there was time for the children to work on their projects. Emily Jane used to hate this time of day, before she had started her crocodile project. Now she looked forward to it! That morning she decided to write about the "saltie" crocodile that she had seen in the mangrove swamps. There was so much to tell! She started drawing a picture of the oysters clinging to the mangroves, and while she drew, she had what she called "a big thinkfulness". She thought about Ayisha and baby Fatou and how different life was for them. Fatou would never know her father. Would she be able to go to school when she grew up? Would she ever learn about Jesus and how he could be her friend and help her with everything? Emily Jane's mother had told her that most of the people in The Gambia did not know the love of Jesus. That was one reason that her Auntie Lucy had gone to work there, so that as well as helping poor people who were sick, she could also tell them about God who cared about them and still did miracles today.

She thought about her class at school and how much they cared about her father's progress. She was so pleased they had made the big card for him. They had prayed in assembly. She had such a nice school, so much nicer than the one Claude had told her about. Even though she was one of the poorer children in the class and didn't have all the latest fashions, the latest computer games or mobile phone or the sort of boots she so wanted, not many of the class bullied her about it. True, there were always some who made fun of her, but most of the class were her friends. She had a really nice teacher who helped her, and she had begun to like doing school work, for the first time ever.

In her head, Emily Jane quietly said a "thank you" to Jesus. Since she had said sorry to him for being angry about her father's accident, she found she liked to talk to him as her friend.

Emily Jane also thought about Jenna. She really was her best friend, but she had been very relieved when her shoes did not fit her, which wasn't very kind. She decided that she would tell Jenna her secret, even if she did laugh at her.

It was soon time to put away the project folders. The picture of the mangrove swamp and the oysters looked good, and there was a "saltie" showing its face coming out of the water. Mrs Brown had remarked that it was a very good piece of work, and was certain to get a merit award for it. Emily Jane beamed. This project was great fun! If only Mrs Brown knew the truth of how she had learnt so much!

Once lunch was over, the girls gathered in groups in the playground. Most of the boys liked to play football, but the girls preferred to chat. "I want to tell you something," Emily Jane said to Jenna. "Let's go and sit on a bench."

"OK," replied Jenna, "Is it about your dad?"

"No actually, it's about my birthday shoes," said Emily

Jane, "I wanted to tell you about them before, but I thought you would laugh at me and think I was telling lies."

"Whatever is it?" asked Jenna, "You make it sound so mysterious!"

"Well, they are magic!" Emily Jane looked at her friend to see if she was laughing at her.

"What do you mean, 'magic'?"

"Well, I can only think that they are magic, because whenever I put them on, something strange happens."

"Go on, tell me more," urged Jenna.

"Well, you won't laugh at me, will you? And please, this is just our secret, between us only. Please promise me that."

"OK, I promise."

"As you know," began Emily Jane, "my Auntie Lucy sent me those shoes for my birthday. I was so angry! I thought they were horrible. Whoever would wear such awful, shiny, pretend crocodile skin shoes? And with a T-bar too! I was so disappointed because I wanted trendy boots like yours. I was in a right strop, I can tell you. Eventually, curiosity or something came over me and I tried them on. The minute I had both shoes on, my eyes became so heavy and I drifted away and woke up in Africa!"

"Wait a minute," interrupted Jenna. "You were just having a dream."

"That's what I thought at first, but it didn't happen just once. It has happened every time I have put them on. It's really strange because I am actually in a real place in Africa and talking to real people and always in a place where there are crocodiles! That's how I came to choose to do a crocodile project – I have been learning so much about them. On one trip I saw a nest with eggs in it, and watched the baby crocodiles hatch! In the 'dream' or whatever it is, when I take the shoes off, for any reason, then I am instantly back at home!"

"Wow!" said Jenna. "Tell me about these dreams. I want to hear more!"

"You do believe me, don't you?" asked Emily Jane, looking at her friend's face to make sure she wasn't laughing at her.

"It's kind of strange but, yes, I do believe you. Anyway you seem to know so much about crocodiles and even Mrs Brown said it was almost as if you had been to Africa!"

Emily Jane was relieved, so began. "My first trip was to Uganda. I was on the shores of Lake Victoria, at the source of the River Nile, and I met a girl called Grace. Then, the second and third times, I was with a boy called Claude in Rwanda, beside a lake near the border with Burundi. Last time I was in The Gambia, in a creek with a lady and her baby daughter."

Jenna's eyes were huge with surprise. "I wish I could come with you on a trip!" she said, "but my feet are too big for your shoes. Remember I tried them on and they didn't fit?"

"I know," said Emily Jane. "At first I was pleased because I wanted to keep my secret all to myself, but then I felt bad about that, because you are my best friend and we have always shared our secrets. That's why I wanted to tell you today. I was a bit afraid that you wouldn't believe me and make fun of me, because it is hard to believe."

"Thank you for sharing your secret, I promise I'll keep it," replied Jenna.

"When I was talking to Claude, I learnt how poor his school is, that is, when he is able to go. Often there is no money for him to go to school, even though he wants to learn, so he can get a good job. They have to pay to go to school there, and if they haven't got any money, they can't go! I've been thinking about it and wondered if maybe I could raise some money to help children like him. Have you any ideas?"

Jenna looked very thoughtful, then came up with an idea. "Well, we could have a table top sale one Saturday. We could sell some of our old toys and things. I could ask my mum to bake some cakes and we could sell those, too. Her cup cakes are out of this world!"

"That's a great idea!" replied Emily Jane enthusiastically. "My mum makes lovely fudge, and coconut ice. I'm sure she would make some to sell. Let's ask our parents when we get home!"

After school, Emily Jane mentioned the thought to her mum, who phoned Jenna's mum. Both were delighted to help the girls with what they agreed was a very good plan. The first thing to do was to set a date, and they decided to have a sale in two weeks' time. That gave everybody time to sort out unwanted items, make things to sell and to advertise around the neighbourhood.

At the church youth club that evening, Emily Jane told the leader there, who also came up with the idea of holding the sale in the church hall. Teas and coffees could be served to the customers, and that would make a little more money. And so it was all arranged that very day!

Emily Jane and Jenna told Mrs Brown about their idea too. She was enthusiastic about the girls wanting to help children in need and said she would allow them to make posters and flyers on the school computer, and also ask the headmaster to tell the whole school about the sale at the next assembly.

Lots of children promised to bring toys for sale and even some parents offered to help! One mother brought some home-made marmalade to be sold, and another some cards which she had made. It was really exciting to see all the lovely things piling up in Emily Jane's hall, ready to be sold.

The two girls were very excited when the Saturday of the sale dawned. They were glad they could use the church hall, because they had so many things to sell! There were toys of all shapes and sizes, a few good-as-new clothes, books and magazines, CDs and DVDs, some pretty vases and ornaments, and wonderful cakes, sweets, biscuits and jams which people had made.

Jenna and Emily Jane helped to put the items out on the tables, so that everything was displayed nicely, then they helped to set the tables ready for people to sit down and have cups of tea. When they had finished, everyone agreed how very good it all looked!

So many people came to the sale from school, church and the neighbourhood that the hall was packed out with people and all the helpers were busy! The girls helped to sell the goods, Emily Jane's dad took the money and the two mothers were having a job just keeping up with pouring out enough cups of tea for the guests!

Finally, the last customer had gone, the washing up had been done and almost all the goods were sold! Emily Jane hovered over her dad while he counted up the money. When he had finished counting, he gave a low whistle.

"We have raised over £1,000!" he shouted. "Thank you and well done to everybody, especially Jenna and Emily Jane," he added. "It just shows that no one is too young to make a difference, I am proud of you both!"

It had been such an exciting day! As they went home, both girls were saying it was the best day they could remember for such a long time. Already they were planning other ways to raise money in the future!

At bedtime, Emily Jane was so tired. She had worked hard all day. She was almost too tired to think, but she wondered how they would get the money to Africa. She must ask Dad about that in the morning. She was sure he would know a way. She yawned, and was just about to get into bed when she remembered. She had prayed to God and asked for lots of money from the sale. He had heard and answered so she must say thank you. She closed her eyes and quietly whispered, "Thank you so much, Lord Jesus, for helping us. Amen."

Emily Jane had meant to put on her birthday shoes before she went to sleep, because she wanted to go and see one of her African friends and tell them the good news, but she was so tired, she fell asleep before she could put them on.

Her parents were exhausted, too. Downstairs they also thanked God for all that the day had held. They thanked Him that their daughter was growing up wanting to help other people. They also thanked God, because in the sale, they had found some high-heeled boots that were exactly what Emily Jane wanted and were her size! It was another miracle!

ELEVEN

Emily Jane's Boots

When Emily Jane woke up the next morning she sat up in bed and hugged her knees. The thought of all the money they had raised filled her with such joy! It would really make a difference in Africa, and she was so happy about that.

Mum came in to see if she was awake, and to tell her breakfast was ready. Her dad was already dressed and downstairs in his wheelchair.

"One day soon, Dad won't need his wheelchair," thought Emily Jane as she ran downstairs. She went to the dining room table and was surprised to see a neatly wrapped shoe box on the table, next to her plate.

"What's this?" she asked.

"At the sale, we found something we knew you would love, so we bought it for you," said her dad. "Open it and see!"

Emily Jane tore off the paper and found the boots! They were perfect! Gasping in delight, she tried them on. They fitted exactly! She danced around the room in them! It was almost unbelievable! She ran to her dad and then to her mum, hugging and kissing them both.

When she stopped dancing around the room, she went back to the table and sat down for breakfast.

"Can I pray today, Dad?" she asked.

"Of course, dear, go ahead."

"Dear God, I want to say a big thank you for these lovely boots. I am so pleased with them, but thank you even more, for the money from the sale that will help the poor children like Claude, Grace and Fatou. Amen."

"Who are you talking about?" asked her mum, when she had stopped praying.

"Some children in Africa who I have learnt about," she answered. "Knowing about them made me want to raise some money." Her parents thought she must have learnt about the children at school or Sunday School, so didn't question her further. Emily Jane was relieved because she did not want to lie to her parents!

"Dad," she asked, "I've been wondering, how do we get the money to Africa to the children?"

"We could send it to The Gambia for Auntie Lucy to give to the poor children there. What do you think about that?" her father answered.

"Could we send some to Rwanda and to Uganda, too?"

"If that is what you and Jenna want, then I am sure we can find the way to do that," he answered. "Now it's about time to go to church. I think everyone there will want to hear how the sale went, and you can wear your boots! I think you might need them because the forecast said it could snow!"

"Jenna says she is coming to Sunday School today, too. She's going to meet us outside," said Emily Jane.

"That is fantastic!" said Mum. "You will enjoy having your best friend there, and you can show her your boots too!" True to her word, Jenna was waiting at the church gate, ready to go to Sunday School with Emily Jane. She noticed the new boots at once!

"Wow! Those boots are great!" she said in surprise. "But it's not your birthday, where did you get them?"

"Mum found them at the sale, wasn't that amazing! They fit perfectly and are nearly new!" replied Emily Jane. "I think it's another miracle!" The girls laughed together as Emily Jane took Jenna in and showed her where to sit.

In Sunday School that morning, the Bible story was about a boy and his lunch. A whole crowd of over 5,000 people had been listening all day to Jesus teach, and at the end of it everyone was hungry. Nobody had any food, or enough money to go and buy some for so many people. Then a little boy offered his packed lunch. It wasn't much at all, just five small rolls and two small fish. But Jesus accepted the boy's gift, thanked God for it, then broke it into pieces and passed it round . . . and there was enough to feed everybody. Not just enough, but when the disciples went round with baskets afterwards, they filled 12 baskets with scraps left over!

Jenna had never heard this story before. At first she

just couldn't believe that Jesus could make that small packed lunch into enough food to feed 5,000!

Then the teacher began to explain that the point of the story was not just the fact that Jesus could do miracles, but also that he can take the little we give him, and make something wonderful out of it.

"Like our little idea of a sale," said Emily Jane, "which grew into a lot of money for the children in Africa."

"Yes, exactly like that," agreed her teacher. "You wanted to do something to help children there, and you didn't think, 'I'm too young' or 'There's nothing I can do'. Like the little boy, you did what you could and Jesus turned it into a miracle."

"That's great," said Jenna. "So Emily Jane was right when she told me that miracles still happen today."

"Yes," agreed the teacher, "but sometimes the Lord uses people, boys and girls and grown ups, to help do the miracles. Not that he needs us, but he wants us to trust him and love him and give our lives to him."

"I think I know what you mean," said Emily Jane to her teacher. "The feelings coming back into my dad's legs are God's miracle. But Dad has had to work hard to learn to walk again and the physiotherapists need to keep helping him."

Jenna was still thinking about the bread rolls and the fish. "Jesus had said thank you to God for that food, before he did the miracle. Is that why some people say a thank you prayer before they eat?"

"Yes, Jenna," said the teacher, "If Jesus said thank you, why shouldn't we? So many people in this world will have no meal today, or very little to eat. It's good to remember to thank God for the food we have."

At the end of the morning, Jenna's mum was waiting in the car outside the church. "Did you enjoy yourself?" she asked.

"It was fun. We had a story about a boy who gave his lunch to Jesus. We talked a lot about it and now I want to say thank you to God before I eat my meals."

"Well," laughed her mum, "that will mean you can't grumble when you have to eat something you don't like!"

Jenna laughed, too, but then she thought, "Actually, that's true. I shouldn't be so fussy about what I eat when so many people have nothing."

Emily Jane helped push her dad home. It was a cold day; snow was forecast, and the pushing helped to warm her up! As she pushed, she had one of her "thinkfulnesses". Her Sunday School teacher had talked about giving their lives to Jesus. She was thinking about the sale, and how it had sprung from her "visits" to Africa, when she put on her birthday shoes. She had just wanted to help the children whom she had met, but she had not thought that it might have been something Jesus wanted her to do. Before her visits to Africa, she had never really thought that Jesus was interested in her life or that he bothered about what she did. Did he really want her life? What did it mean to "give your life to Jesus"? If she gave it to him, what would he do with it?

As she tried to figure it all out in her mind, it was as if other thoughts were there, too, telling her that she was just a child and that Jesus really wasn't bothered about her.

Then she remembered a song she used to sing in Sunday School when she was little, "Jesus loves the little children, all the children of the world . . ." It was as if a little voice in her head was reminding her, "Of course Jesus is bothered about you. Didn't he arrange for a pair of boots to be in the sale which were just what you wanted and fitted you perfectly?" Then the other voice argued, "If he really cared, then he would have healed your dad long ago, and he would have had enough money to buy them for you on your birthday!"

Emily Jane thought about what her Sunday School teacher had said. Jesus could heal someone instantly, but sometimes he chose to use other people to help and work with him. That seemed to make sense, but by the time they arrived home, her head was in a complete whirl.

"My princess is very quiet and thoughtful today," remarked her dad, as she helped to make him comfortable on his chair. "What's going on in her pretty head?"

"Lots of things. It's hard to explain," replied Emily Jane. "I have been thinking about miracles and something my teacher said this morning. I don't really understand what it means when she tells us we need to give our lives to Jesus."

Her dad looked thoughtful. "You know, before we are even born, Jesus knows all about us and loves us. He already has a wonderful plan for our lives. However, we have to come to hear about his love and believe that it is true, before we can trust him to work out the plans. Mostly, we want to run our own lives and do things our own way. We mess things up and get it all wrong. That means we sin. People sometimes don't like using that word these days, but it is the Bible word for when we do wrong things and make God sad. We deserve to be punished, but God sent Jesus to come and be a person just like us, but he never did anything wrong. Then he died, instead of us. He took the punishment that we should have."

Emily Jane thought about it. "Like if I lose a library book, you and mum pay for it, because I haven't got any money."

Dad smiled. "Exactly! Giving our lives to Jesus means that we realise that we need to be forgiven by God for the wrong in our lives, and asking Jesus to make us clean and to be the boss in our lives, rather than us. Then we try to live our lives by asking him what he wants, and trying to do what he would want us to do. We still get it wrong sometimes, but we can always say sorry and ask for help to get it right. We find out more and more of what Jesus wants for our lives as we read the Bible and have people teach us, like your Sunday School teacher. Does that help?"

"Yes, I think so," answered Emily Jane. "Thank you for explaining. Would you like to play a game with me now?"

"In a little while, first I am going to do my exercises. Do you want to stay and help me?" Dad replied.

"Of course!" answered Emily Jane.

"First, could you bring me the walking frame that's in the hall and put it in front of the wheelchair, for me, please?" The walking frame had been in the hall for a couple of days, but Emily Jane hadn't really thought much about it or what it might be used for. She was used to so many pieces of medical equipment around the house, that she didn't bother to ask why they were there. She did as her father had asked and fetched the frame, putting it in front of his chair. She was so excited when she watched him pull himself up on to his feet and hold on to the frame.

"Now watch this!" Dad said, "I have been practising this as a surprise to show you this weekend." He slowly pushed the frame along, moving first one foot and then the other. Emily Jane danced around in joy! She was shouting to her mother, telling her to come and see. Her mum came running in, wondering what was happening.

As they watched Dad take his steps, tears started to run down her mum's face. They were tears of happiness. Emily Jane found that she had tears, too! They had longed for this day for many years, and it was so wonderful.

"Dad," said Emily Jane, "one day you will be able to walk everywhere!"

"One of these days I will walk into church, and we will all praise God for his miracle of healing!" he replied.

"I can't wait! Can I tell them at school, because they pray for you in assembly sometimes?"

"Of course."

Soon they were all sitting down to Sunday roast, feeling very cheerful. Mum said the thank you prayer for the food, and Emily Jane really did feel grateful when she looked at the roast chicken and lovely vegetables on her plate. She didn't know that a few blocks away in her home, Jenna was also saying thank you in front of her astonished mum!

As Emily Jane helped to clear away the dinner plates, she noticed out of the corner of her eye that it had begun to snow! She gasped in astonishment as her mum suddenly said, "Goodness! It is snowing hard. If this keeps up school will be closed tomorrow!"

Emily Jane ran over to the window to get a better look. How beautiful the flakes looked as they swirled and fell. If there was enough, perhaps she and Jenna could play in it tomorrow!

A SNOWY DAY

A Snowy Day

When Emily Jane woke up the next morning there was a strange light coming through the window. She quickly pulled the curtains and gasped in awe. Everything was covered in a blanket of thick white snow! It was so beautiful, just like fairyland!

"School is closed today because of the snow," her mum told her when she ran downstairs. Emily Jane gave a whoop of delight. It would be such fun to have a day off school and play in the snow! She phoned Jenna to see if she could come round.

"I have a better idea," said Jenna. "I have a sledge and we could go up to the park and sledge down the bank! Put your wellies on, not your new boots or they will get spoilt!"

It was fantastic fun sledging down the bank in the park. Loads of other young people were there, and they had snowball fights, too! All too soon it was lunch time and they had to go home. It was nearly the end of February and half term would soon be here. Jenna wondered if the snow would last until then. What fun they would have if it did!

After lunch Emily Jane realised she was tired. So much had happened over the last few days! There had been all the excitement of the sale, Jenna coming to church, Dad walking, and now the fun in the snow! She decided to go to her room and read a book. She looked on her bookshelf for something interesting to read, but then she saw the box with her birthday shoes.

"I'll put them on and maybe I can see Grace or Claude or Ayisha and tell them about the table sale and the money," she said to herself. As she got the box down from the shelf, she had a sudden thought. "If I go to Africa today, I will be too hot in all these clothes! So she took off her thick jumper and shivered a little in her T-shirt, before she put on her shoes.

The dreamy feeling instantly came over her, and she found that she was once again standing near a lake. "Am I back at Jinja?" she wondered. All she could see was a great expanse of water, but somehow it didn't look like Lake Victoria. The shore was sandy, but then there were steep banks with scrubby bushes growing on them. Near the shore, trees with large orange fruit were growing. At first Emily Jane thought the fruit were oranges, but as she looked closer she realised they were too large – they were mangoes! Suddenly a screech up in the trees made her jump! What was that? Looking up, she saw that it was a monkey with a long brown and black tail swinging among the branches. Fascinated, Emily Jane continued to watch him. She was so engrossed that she didn't notice a group of children coming down the bank towards the shore. They were chattering away. Suddenly the children made a circle around her and Emily Jane felt scared. They were looking at her as if she was a strange creature from Mars! The children looked about her age, but all of them seemed very thin. Their skin looked grey rather than brown, and they all had shaved heads. Their clothes were really ragged and old. One of the children reached out and touched her hair, then another her arm. Emily Jane didn't know what to do or to say. Then she remembered her mother had always told her to be polite and greet people.

"Hello," she said. "I hope you can understand me. My name is Emily Jane." The children then began to chatter again, smiling at her. Although she didn't understand their language, she could understand what they were saying, just as she had when she met Claude.

"Where do you live?" one of the biggest boys asked her. "You do not live here in our village of Kasengu. Have you come from the town of Bunia? Have you run away because of the fighting?"

"I live a long way away in a country called England," said Emily Jane, wondering where on earth she was today! It was certainly different from snowy England! It was not sunny, but very hot and humid and the sky was covered with thick grey clouds, as if a storm might break at any moment.

"Don't you live in Congo like us?" a girl asked. "Yet you are brown and not white skinned. You are strange though, and have pretty hair and shiny skin. We have come to swim, so that we can get clean. Now it is the rainy season we get very muddy and dirty."

Emily Jane looked at the girl's skin and saw that it was grey because it was covered in dry mud. She counted quickly and saw that there were eight children in the group.

"Do you want to swim with us?" another child asked. "It should be safe, because one of us always stays on the shore as a look out for crocodiles, and another up on the bank to look out for danger. We take it in turns to swim and get clean."

"I don't know if I want to swim," said Emily Jane. "I had a shower after playing in the snow this morning."

"Snow?" asked one of the children, "What is snow?"

Emily Jane laughed, realising that these children would have no idea what it was! She tried to explain, pointing to the clouds in the sky, that where she lived it was so cold at the moment that instead of rain, the clouds dropped cold, white flakes called snow, which stayed on the cold ground. She could see the children had no idea what she meant, but laughed at the idea of thick, cold white stuff on the ground.

"Can I stay with your lookout on the shore?" she asked.

"Yes," said a girl, "It's me. My name is Penina. Stay

and talk with me. Antoine will go up the bank. He has good eyes!"

The other six children stripped off their top clothes and ran into the water. Emily Jane was glad to be able to ask Penina questions.

"Why are you the look out?" she asked, "What are you looking for?"

"Well," Penina answered, "This year the rains have come early and are very heavy. Usually the months of January and February are very hot and dry. That is why school is closed for most of those weeks. It is our long holiday. Not that we all go to school, but some of us do," she added. "This Lake Albert belongs half to our country of Congo and over there," she said pointing into the distance, "the other half belongs to Uganda. It is a good lake, full of fish. Usually we have no trouble and we can swim safely, but this year the rains have brought flooding. The flooding means the shore is smaller than usual. The lake has become disturbed, and so have the lake creatures including the crocodiles. They are unhappy and now very dangerous. They have been known to eat children in flood times, so one of us always keeps watch while the others swim."

"Goodness," said Emily Jane, thinking how glad she was that she had decided not to swim.

Penina nodded. "It is a bit scary, but we need to keep clean. It's OK if we keep our eyes open. See, I look at the water to notice if there are any strange ripples or things that look like logs. The children all keep together and make a lot of noise. That way they feel safer. We have nowhere else to wash properly and it is fun in the water!"

Emily Jane agreed. She could see the children were having a great time splashing around. Soon a boy came to replace Penina as the look out, so that she could swim.

"I am Josephu," he told Emily Jane. "It is a terrible thing when the floods come and disturb the crocodiles. Usually they live far out in the lake and we can swim without fear, but these are bad days. The seasons for rain and dry are all muddled up and it makes it bad for us, and for the crops, too. We never know if we will have floods or drought."

As they were talking, a screech suddenly pierced the air. It was a shrill noise, like a scared monkey. As soon as they heard it the children ran out of the water and headed towards a clump of trees, running as fast as they could. The screech had come from Antoine. He had cleverly copied the monkey's screech, and that was the signal for danger! Josephu grabbed Emily Jane's hand.

"Run!" he said, urgently. "Run! I will help you. We must escape."

Antoine, the look out on the bank, having alerted everyone to danger, was running too. In silence, the children headed into the trees and Josephu ran with Emily Jane guiding her through the tree roots until they reached a cave. The entrance was so well hidden by tree branches, Emily Jane would not have known it was there if she had been on her own. She was out of breath and very scared, not knowing why they were running and hiding. The cave was very dark and Josephu led her deep inside. Finally, when he felt it was safe, he said quietly, "Sorry to make you run. We will have to stay here for some time. We can talk, but quietly. Then we shall remain safe."

"What are we hiding from? What is the danger?" asked Emily Jane.

"You do not know! Of course, you live in white people's land, even though you have brown skin. We are hiding from rebel soldiers. Our land has had war for many years. Not the whole country, but in this part. These rebel soldiers kidnap children and make them their slaves. Although they hunt for us, they have never found our hiding place. No child has been snatched from Kisengu!"

In the cave the other children were shivering, having run out of the lake without drying themselves. Josephu went to the side of the cave where the children had a few old blankets. He seemed to be the eldest and the leader of the group. He quickly gave them out and the children who were wet wrapped themselves up to get warm. They wished they had some food but they couldn't store food in the cave because of rats and other wild creatures that might find and eat it.

"How long will you have to stay here?" Emily Jane asked Josephu.

"Usually we stay until it is dark. The rebels will have given up searching long before then and we can get home safely."

"Won't your parents be worried?" Emily Jane asked.

"Some of us are orphans from the war and live on our own in the village. Others, well, the adults in the village all know that we run to hide if we sense danger. They don't ask us where we go, so that, if they are questioned they cannot give away our hiding place. No one except those of us in here knows about this cave. It is best that way. Please keep our secret, won't you?"

Emily Jane felt very important when she was trusted to keep the secret. She was feeling less scared now in the company of these brave and kind children. She was so sad to think that they had to live their lives in this way. It shocked her to realise that some of the children who were about her age or younger had to look after themselves because they were orphans.

"Of course you can trust me," she said. "I will never reveal your secret."

The children, once they were feeling warmer, began to sing softly. Emily Jane's eyes had become accustomed to the dark and she could see their bright eyes and smiling faces as they swayed in time to the music.

"What are you singing?" Emily Jane asked them.

"We are singing thanks to God that he has kept us

safe," replied Penina. "We have a church in our village and we love to sing and dance at the services as well as hear more about God who is our Father. We pray together each morning and ask him to take care of us and protect us. He really does look after us."

"I pray to him, too," said Emily Jane.

"That is very good," said Penina. "Can you sing a song to us in your language?"

Emily Jane had to think quickly. She decided to sing a song that she had learnt at school. "Jesus loves the little children," she sang. The children very quickly picked up the words and the tune and sang along with her in their own language! They seemed so happy. Nobody would have thought that they were a group of children in hiding!

What a day it had been! Emily Jane thought of all the fun she had with Jenna in the park sledging and playing snowballs, and then going on an adventure to the Congo in the afternoon!

Suddenly she was feeling very sleepy. She undid her shoes and drifted into sleep. She woke up on top of her bed at home.

THIRTEEN

The Miracle Pool at Katchikally

The next few weeks seemed to pass very quickly for Emily Jane. Half term came and went, and with it, the cold weather. Suddenly spring had arrived, and the whole world seemed to wake up from winter's sleep. She loved finding the first primroses in the garden. She also loved wearing her new boots to school. Her father went to the hospital most days now, and his legs were getting much stronger. Sometimes at home he walked with the frame, instead of using the wheelchair!

The crocodile project was almost finished. Emily Jane was proud of it; she had done some great writing and lovely drawings to illustrate the writing. Soon it would be ready to show to the headmaster. She loved to look at all the work and think about Grace, Claude, Ayisha, Fatou, Penina, Josephu and the other children she had met. She wondered how they were getting on. She kept promising herself that one day soon she would try on her birthday shoes again and see if the magic still worked. Even Jenna had asked her recently if she had worn them, but the days had been so busy with all the activities at school, and after school she often spent time with her dad, helping him walk around the house. Emily Jane was helping him so that when Auntie Lucy came to visit in the Easter holidays, they could give her a big surprise, and she could see him walk!

One Saturday in March, Emily Jane woke up and felt dreary. Opening the curtains, she saw that it was pouring with rain and the sky was covered with thick, grey clouds, not like the beautiful sunshine they had been having.

Emily Jane felt disappointed. She had planned to go out with Jenna to the park. She lay on her bed feeling very grumpy. In her head the words, "It's not fair" were going round and round. It was a long time since she had felt so fed up and in such a bad mood.

Mum called her to come down for breakfast and she snapped back at her. Then Emily Jane felt really awful, because she knew it wasn't her mum's fault that it was a wet day! She got up and went downstairs to have her breakfast, now feeling cross with herself as well as everyone else! She didn't feel like saying thank you to God for her food, or thank you for anything else either. She ate her cereal and toast in silence.

"What are you planning to do today?" asked her father.

"I don't know, nothing much, it's raining too hard," she replied in quite a grumpy voice. Her mum said, "Well it would help me if you tidied up your room today. I want to give it a good clean on Monday."

"Do I *have* to?" Emily Jane moaned.

"Yes," answered her mother, "you do!" So Emily Jane stomped up the stairs, making sure everyone heard that she was in a strop. She started to tidy up her clothes. Even she had to admit her room had got into a mess. She was not the most tidy person in the world! Then she started on her games, and even began to enjoy herself sorting them out. She sorted her DVDs and when she saw *The Secret Garden* she thought perhaps she could ask Jenna to come around later on and watch it with her. It was still her favourite film. Finally, she saw her shoe box with the birthday shoes.

"Will the magic still work?" she wondered. "I don't even know if the shoes will still fit me!" There was only one way to know the answer. Emily Jane reached and pulled the box down from the shelf where she kept them. They even looked a little dusty. She found a tissue and polished them, then sitting on her bed, feeling just a bit nervous, she pulled off her slippers and gently put one foot into a shoe. It was a really tight fit! Then she just managed to squeeze the second foot into the other shoe. As she did so, she felt her eyes becoming so heavy she could not keep them open.

Emily Jane found herself in a village or a town, with houses everywhere and paths running between them. Not a lake or crocodile in sight, but it did still look and feel like Africa! There were people everywhere, hustling and bustling, and children running around. The houses were square, most of them with whitewashed, cement walls and corrugated iron roofs. They looked quite smart compared with some of the other houses Emily Jane had seen in Africa. Outside some of the houses there were pictures made of painted cloth, hanging to dry on wooden frames. Some of the other houses had tables outside which were covered with African crafts. Walking closer so she could have a better look, Emily Jane noticed that they had price tags on them. There were carved animals, brightly woven baskets and lots of pretty jewellery. People started to call to her.

"Come and buy from me! I have lovely things at a good price!" Emily Jane had no money, but she walked over to the nearest house and admired the beautiful paintings. A girl about her age came over and spoke to her in English.

"These are made by my mother. Do you like them?"

"They are beautiful!" answered Emily Jane in admiration. "How does she make them?"

"Come and see," said the girl, leading her through the small house and into the back yard. There a lady was drawing a picture on a large piece of cloth.

"Now Mum will go over the lines with hot wax," explained the girl, who had told Emily Jane that her name was Isatou.

"Next she will paint within the lines and the wax will stop the paint going to any other part of the cloth. When it is all painted in different colours, it will be washed and dried and ironed, and be ready to be sold. It is called 'batik' work. My mum also does 'tie and dye' patterns on plain material. People buy the cloth to make clothes. She makes the best fabric around!"

Emily Jane watched as Isatou's mother painted a picture of a crocodile lying asleep by a pool.

"This is our favourite picture and one which sells the best," said Isatou. "Tourists like to buy it, when they visit the Katchikally sacred crocodile pool."

"Where is that?" asked Emily Jane, "I have never heard of it before."

"Why, it is here. This is Katchikally village! You must know about the pool!"

"I don't," replied Emily Jane, feeling rather foolish. "I'm not quite sure about anything, even which country I am in!"

"You are silly. You must know you are in The Gambia! Did you come by plane or do you live here?" asked Isatou.

"I live in England, but my auntie lives here," said Emily Jane in amazement, realising that if this was The Gambia, she must be close to Auntie Lucy!

The girls could hear a lot of noise outside the house, so Isatou grabbed Emily Jane's hand and they ran to see what was happening. Tourists were pouring out of a coach which had pulled up. Most of them had white skin and were speaking English, but with an American accent.

"They have come to see the crocodiles," said Isatou. "Let's walk along with them and we can go in to the pool."

Emily Jane wasn't sure if it was right to do this, but before she knew what was happening, she was dragged into the crowd of visitors by Isatou and nobody seemed to mind at all. They entered the gate and walked along the path until they came to a small lake. Well, Emily Jane decided that it was really a large pond, completely covered by weed, which made it totally green.

"This is the sacred pool," said Isatou in a whisper. "Look around the shores, some of the crocodiles are sunbathing. Inside the pool, under the plants, are about one hundred crocodiles. They cannot be killed, they are sacred."

Emily Jane looked around her, and almost screamed in fear! Hundreds of huge crocodiles, well camouflaged, lazed around the pool in the sun. Some had to be at least five metres long!

The tourists were being encouraged to touch them, and have their photographs taken as they did so. Emily Jane shuddered!

Isatou saw the horrified look on her face and explained that they were so well fed every day that they would not attack people and that it was quite safe to touch them. After a great deal of persuasion, Emily Jane did go near to one of the crocodiles and reached out her hand and touched it. It felt a bit cold, but softer than she expected.

She looked down at her shoes, and whispered, "I don't quite know what to say to you, crocodile, but I do like my shoes because they are not made of crocodile skin. I am so glad no crocodile was killed to make them."

Isatou nodded. "Fake skin is better," she agreed.

"Why are these crocodiles sacred?" Emily Jane asked her new friend.

"It's a long story, a fable really about lovers, but it is said that if any woman who can't have babies visits here, then within a year she should find that she has become pregnant. She's supposed to swim with the crocodiles, but it's not allowed any more. Even though it is just a fable, many African women come because they hope that the magic might work for them." Isatou took a deep breath. "Even some of the American tourists believe it. I used to believe it too, but just recently something happened which changed my life."

"Oh, what was that?" asked Emily Jane.

Isatou gave a big sigh. "One day my dad got a new wife. I hated to see my mother treated so unfairly and so unkindly. She may not be so young or look so pretty now, but she is good and kind and you saw what lovely batik paintings she does. I hated the new wife and wanted to harm her. The feelings of hate were getting stronger and stronger and I was very miserable. Then, a friend at school saw how upset and angry I was and asked me why. She was the first person who listened to me. It helped me just to talk to her. She asked if she could pray with me because she was a Christian. I didn't see why not, so I said, 'yes'. Every day at lunch time she took me to a quiet place and said a prayer for me, asking God that I would know the love of Jesus instead of the hate that was in my heart. Gradually I began to feel different inside. It is hard to explain, but I began to look forward to praying with her so much. I didn't understand very well, but one day I asked Jesus to come into my life and fill it with love. This wonderful feeling inside of me grew and has never gone away. The bitterness and hate I felt towards the second wife is going. That is what the love of God does; he helps us to love and not to hate."

Isatou looked at Emily Jane and asked her, "What about you? Are you a Christian, too?"

Emily Jane hesitated for a minute before answering.

"I've always gone to church with my mum and dad, since I was a baby. Then my dad had an accident and couldn't walk any more and I used to be angry with God about that. My dad's getting better now though, and that really is a miracle. Recently I have been praying and asking God things. I still go to church and Sunday School, but I don't think I've ever really asked Jesus into my life. I talked to my dad one day and he explained about what it meant, but I never did it. So, I guess I am not really a Christian inside, like you are."

The girls were sitting on a log very close to a crocodile, which was sleeping on the warm earth. Emily

Jane thought about all the things that had happened to her since the day she was given the birthday shoes, and it seemed to her that in all her adventures, God had been showing her what she needed to do. Could there be a better time or place to pray and ask Jesus into her life than right here beside a crocodile? Emily Jane thought back to earlier that morning when she had been so grumpy and rude to her mum. She was sorry about that. There were so many things she felt bad about.

"You can ask Jesus in to your life any time, if you want to," Isatou encouraged her.

So Emily Jane closed her eyes and whispered a prayer to Jesus, asking for forgiveness and asking him to come and be part of her life, to be her "boss", like her dad had said. And she knew that Jesus did so. How can you explain these things? You can't really, you have to experience them.

She took Isatou's hand and squeezed it. "Thank you Isatou, you have helped me so much today. I have now asked Jesus to come into my life, too."

The girls sat there in the warm sun, and the crocodile opened its eyes and seemed to smile at them.

"Look at my birthday shoes!" Emily Jane said to the reptile, and took them off to show him.

Back in her bedroom, Emily Jane lay on her bed very quietly. She knew she had left Katchikally behind and that her birthday shoes would never fit her again. In fact, she didn't need them any more. Her adventures had taught her many things about Africa and crocodiles, but far more than that, they had helped her to find out how to give her life to Jesus. A kind of gentle warmth still filled her and she knew that whether it was a dream or whether she really had been in The Gambia, her prayer had been from her heart and the Lord had answered it.

She was now a Christian.

After that special day, Emily Jane put her birthday shoes away. She knew she had grown out of them, but wanted to keep them for ever as a reminder of all her magic adventures in Africa. She wrapped them in tissue paper and tied the box with a lovely red satin ribbon. She decided that when she got her project back from Mrs Brown she would put that in the box too, with the promised merit award.

It was a wonderful day when Auntie Lucy came. Emily Jane had been waiting to see her for so long, so she could say a proper thank you for the shoes! Auntie Lucy gave gifts to everybody and Emily Jane gasped in astonishment as she opened hers. It was the exact length of batik fabric with the picture of the crocodile that she had seen Isatou's mother making!

"Thank you, Auntie Lucy, thank you," yelled Emily Jane. "You are the most wonderful present-giver ever! How did you know I wanted this picture? It's almost as good a present as my birthday shoes!"

Her auntie hugged Emily Jane and gave her a big wink. "It's not just a picture! You can wrap it round yourself to make an African-style skirt – shall I show you how?"

Also by Mary Weeks Millard:

I Want to Be an Airline Pilot

Shema, an 8-year-old Rwandan goatherd from a child-led family, has many adventures, including a goat eating his only T-shirt, a frightening visit to a medicine man and a dangerously close brush with a spitting black cobra! Through them all, little by little, Shema learns about "Mister God" and discovers that although he is an orphan, he has a Father in heaven who cares for him.

A victorious heart-warming story for 8–11s, with lovely background to life in rural Rwanda.

"A thrilling adventure story about three orphans' dreams coming true when their prayers were answered." – Jonathan

"I give this book 10/10." – Ellie

"I think this book is very good; it made me feel happy, sad and really excited. I think the most interesting part is when Shema faced the black cobra. It was also very moving when in the book Ishimwe starts to cry because her parents died. I really enjoyed this book. It is one of my favourites."

– Kemi

ISBN: 978 0 9536963 5 2

Also available from Dernier Publishing for girls aged 10–14:

Beech Bank Girls, Every Girl Has a Story
by Eleanor Watkins

Six teenage friends draw nearer to God and to each other
in these fun, moving and honest accounts. Annie, Willow,
Rachel, Holly, Amber and Chloe share their laughter,
their tears, their hopes, their fears and their secrets with
each other and with us. Miracle and party included!

"... a very interesting book, dealing with a number of
situations encountered by teenage girls. ... I really enjoyed
it and found it helpful at the same time." – Claire

ISBN 978 0 9536963 4 5

Beech Bank Girls, Making a Difference
by Eleanor Watkins

The Beech Bank Girls discover that they do not have to
wait until their gap year to start helping people in need.
The friends learn from some tough issues that they *can*
make a difference and have lots of fun at the same time!

"When the girls get into bad situations or dilemmas, they
all get together and pray ... makes you want to read more
and find out what happens next." – Ellie

ISBN 978 0 9536963 7 6

Read the first chapters on our website,
www.dernierpublishing.com

Also from Dernier Publishing for readers aged 8–11:

The Treasure Hunt by J. M. Evans

Ravi, Debbie, Joel and Lance's first exciting mystery adventure. Who is in the back of the white lorry and why are they there? Prayer, faith and their Bible knowledge all help, but when the case takes an unexpected turn, the friends also need to be courageous and obedient. Will they find out what is really going on and find the real treasure?

"This is the best book I've ever read." – Emily

ISBN 978 0 9536963 1 4

Mystery in the Snow by J. M. Evans

Not long after solving their first mystery (*The Treasure Hunt*), Ravi, Debbie, Lance and Joel find themselves with another problem; Ravi's shed has been burgled. Can they find out who did it? The plot thickens as an old lady's handbag goes missing, then a cat disappears. Can all these things be connected? Join the Christian friends as they find answers in unexpected places.

"So exciting that I couldn't put it down." – Lydia

ISBN 978 0 9536963 3 8

Deepest Darkness by Denise Hayward

Ten-year old Abi suffers from terrible nightmares and her life is ruled by fear. On holiday in Canada, she makes a new friend who shows her that true light shines, even in the deepest darkness. Facing her fears one by one, Abi opens her life to the light and finds a freedom that she never thought possible.

A brilliantly-written, gentle, moving story full of adventure.

"This is one of the best books I've read – EVER." – Maddie
"It's a fantastic adventure and God is really real." – Natalie
"I enjoyed the story very much. I felt for Abi and all the characters, and was really excited while reading the book."
– Polina

ISBN 978 0 9536963 6 9

Not sure which book to choose? Read reviews and the first chapters of all our books on our website,
www.dernierpublishing.com

Also from Dernier Publishing for teens:

London's Gone by J. M. Evans

A thrilling teen drama full of suspense.

ISBN 978 0 9536963 2 1

The Only Way by Gareth Rowe

A brilliantly-written tough story of hope and redemption.

ISBN 978 0 9536963 9 0

All Dernier Publishing titles are available from your local
bookshop, on-line book store and direct from
www.dernierpublishing.com